'It's time I said goodnight.'

Luca got up slowly, his eyes holding hers. 'Why? Are you afraid?'

'Not afraid exactly.' She held his gaze as she searched for the right word. 'Prudent? No, wary. That's it. I'm wary…of giving you, or anyone else, the wrong impression.'

Luca moved closer. 'Are you saying that because of this soldier of yours you are immune to me? Or is Tom Hannay the real obstacle?'

Georgia's eyes flashed dark, resentful fire at him. 'Will you stop all this nonsense about Tom?'

'I know I have the power to make you forget him. And all other men… Tell me you are indifferent to me—if you can!'

Catherine George was born in Wales, and early developed a passion for reading which eventually fuelled her compulsion to write. Marriage to an engineer led to nine years in Brazil, but on his later travels the education of her son and daughter kept her in the UK. And instead of constant reading to pass her lonely evenings she began to write the first of her romantic novels. When not writing and reading she loves to cook, listen to opera, browse in antiques shops and walk the Labrador.

Recent titles by the same author:

FALLEN HERO
EARTHBOUND ANGEL

THE RIGHT CHOICE

BY
CATHERINE GEORGE

MILLS & BOON

All the characters in this book have no existence outside the imagination of the author, and have no relation whatsoever to anyone bearing the same name or names. They are not even distantly inspired by any individual known or unknown to the author, and all the incidents are pure invention.

MILLS & BOON and the Rose Device
are trademarks of the publisher.
Harlequin Mills & Boon Limited,
Eton House, 18-24 Paradise Road, Richmond, Surrey TW9 1SR

© Catherine George 1996

ISBN 0 263 79512 8

Set in Times Roman 10½ on 12 pt.
01-9606-53010 C1

Made and printed in Great Britain

CHAPTER ONE

TAKE-OFF, the pilot explained with regret over the intercom, would be a little delayed. The plane bound for Pisa, full except for one aisle-seat halfway down the aircraft, rippled with a frisson of audible nerves from some of the passengers, and smart flight attendants circulated quickly to give reassurances. The delay was due to nothing more alarming than the late arrival of a passenger.

Georgia leaned across the man sandwiched between herself and her sister. 'And here he comes!' Charlotte, half-asleep from the tranquillisers she'd taken, eyed the commotion glumly from her window-seat as a tall, dark-haired man was installed with ceremony across the aisle from Georgia. Two of the female staff helped eagerly as he stowed his hand luggage away, and Georgia stifled a giggle as she listened to the voluble exchange in Italian.

'What's up?' said Tom in an undertone.

She leaned close to whisper in his ear. 'They're apologising for the accommodation. No room in first class. Shame!'

Tom relayed the news to his wife, but a wan smile was Charlotte's only response. Georgia knew that by this stage her sister wanted nothing more than to run from the plane and catch the next train home. The engines began to roar at last, the attendants moved to their places, Tom Hannay took his wife's icy hand and seconds later they were airborne.

5

Georgia sat back in her seat as the plane climbed above the clouds, unafflicted by the nerves her sister suffered. She turned to smile at Tom, relieved to see Charlotte's eyelids drooping. The pills were taking effect, and in minutes, as Georgia knew from experience, her sister would be fast asleep. Once the seatbelt light was off, the late arrival got to his feet and folded an expensive suede jacket into the overhead compartment. As he did so a slim leather wallet plummeted from it into Georgia's lap. She waited until he'd disposed his long legs to his satisfaction, then leaned across and handed back his property.

Gleaming blue eyes met hers with open admiration. '*Grazie!*' he said, smiling, in the deep, gravel-toned accents that Georgia had met often during her dealings with the Italian male. 'It fell from my jacket—I trust you are not hurt?'

'Not at all,' she said coolly.

'I regret I was late,' he went on, undeterred. 'Does the delay cause you inconvenience?'

'No, it doesn't,' she assured him, conscious that Tom was listening with amusement.

'You travel to Pisa only? Or do you go on to Florence?'

Georgia took the flight magazine from its pouch, hoping he'd take the hint. 'To Florence.'

'This is your first visit there?' said the Italian, settling back comfortably in his seat, so obviously prepared to chat that Georgia's hackles rose. Something about the man annoyed her. He was too good-looking, too confident of his own charms, too—everything.

'Yes, it is,' she said shortly, annoyed by his assumption that she was delighted to talk to him.

'You will enjoy it very much,' he stated, half-turned towards her, a hint of intimacy in his attitude which irritated her considerably. 'Firenze is an experience rather than just a town, you understand.'

She gave him a cool little smile, then looked up in relief as the rattle of trolleys put an end to the exchange. She let down her tray ready for the meal on its way to them, and out of the corner of her eye saw the Italian do the same, a wry little smile on his lips.

When the familiar plastic trays arrived Georgia slid a slice of cheese into the bread roll provided, tucked it into a napkin and put it aside. 'Charlotte's appetite usually wakes up when she does!' she murmured to Tom.

'I learned that early on,' he returned with feeling, doing the same. 'When we got to Paris on our wedding day my bride demanded a very late, very large meal via room service before the honeymoon could get off to a proper start.'

Georgia giggled, then frowned as she met the heavy-lidded blue gaze trained on her from across the aisle. She turned away quickly, annoyed to find her colour high, and grateful when a pretty flight attendant arrived to dispense coffee, wine, or anything else the handsome latecomer desired.

'You've made a hit there,' muttered Tom, grinning into his glass of wine.

Georgia sniffed. 'The passengers next to him are men. I was just the nearest female for his chat-up line. He must be a celebrity of some kind, the way the attendants are fluttering round him.'

'Face looks familiar,' he agreed, frowning. 'But I can't place it. Not an actor or something, is he?'

Georgia indulged in a bit of discreet peeping round the duty-free trolley, but the man's face was unfamiliar. 'Certainly got the profile for it,' she whispered. 'Complete with Roman nose.' She caught a glimpse of a long, slim foot in the kind of shoe that Italy was famous for, then the flash of a gold Rolex watch, worn loose on a muscular brown wrist, as the man accepted a refill of coffee. 'He looks used to the *dolce vita*, that's for sure—and to people dancing to his bidding.'

'Shut up, Georgie,' said Tom hastily. 'He'll hear you.'

But a glance at the aquiline profile reassured her. The heavy, black-lashed lids were closed.

The short flight to Pisa was soon over. As they made their descent Charlotte woke up right on cue, passionately grateful to find her ordeal almost over as she devoured the cheese rolls that her companions had saved for her.

The moment the plane touched down the elegant Italian was on his feet and ready for the off. He gave Georgia a dazzling smile and a slight, deliberate bow. '*Arrivederci*! Enjoy your visit.' He slung the suede jacket over one shoulder and made a swift exit from the plane to a send-off of farewells and good wishes from the aircraft attendants and a handshake from the pilot.

'Dear me,' said Charlotte as Tom retrieved their hand luggage. 'Who *was* that, Georgia? Someone important?'

'*He* thought he was,' retorted her sister, grinning.

Charlotte, a different person once the plane had landed, was jubilant as they waited for their baggage in the air terminal. 'Just look at this gorgeous sunshine!' she exclaimed happily. 'And we've got two whole weeks of it, Tom.' She sighed as they made their way to the waiting train. 'A pity you aren't spending more than one night of it with us, Georgie.'

'A job's a job,' said Georgia blithely. 'Besides, Tom, angel though he is, can hardly want me tagging along.'

'Dead right,' said Tom bluntly, grinning to take the edge off his words. 'I love you madly, Georgia Fleming, but I want your sister all to myself.'

'Tom!' said Charlotte, shocked, as the train began to move off. 'What a thing to say.'

'It's true,' said her husband, unabashed.

'Thank you, darling.' They smiled at each other lovingly.

'Now don't go all sloppy on me, you two,' ordered Georgia sternly. 'Have a care for my youth and inexperience.'

Her sister hooted. 'I don't know about the last bit, but you're exactly eleven months younger than me. Mother never spares us grisly tales of her heroism in surviving two babies in nappies.'

Georgia pulled a face. 'Another reason for staying fancy-free a bit longer!'

'Don't you like children?' demanded Tom. 'If not, I pity the poor little beggars you teach.'

'Ah, but I can hand those back to their mothers when school's over for the day!' Georgia laughed. 'Of course I like children—I like babies too. It's the reproduction bit I'm not keen on. Why wasn't I born a man?'

Tom Hannay gave her a long, slow scrutiny. 'The answer to that's obvious.' He put an arm round his wife's waist and touched his lips to her cheek. 'Politically incorrect it may be, but the women in your family

were all meant to be just that—women! Your mother
included,' he added, with a grin.

They arrived at the hotel in a blaze of sunshine which
turned the River Arno into a flowing ribbon of gold
below Georgia's window. She leaned over the balcony
in delight, moving aside tubs of flowers so that she
could stretch to see the Ponte Vecchio in the distance
and drink in the beauty and noise and sheer vitality
of Florence in one great heady, intoxicating draught.

She'd been teaching English near Venice for a whole
academic year already, but her love affair with Italy
merely intensified as she grew to know the country
better. Even the stress and strain of instilling English
into reluctant little heads took none of the gilt off the
gingerbread. She'd spent two working vacations at the
Venice school's summer camp in her student days,
before getting her English degree.

This, indirectly, was responsible for her presence
here right now, in the summer, when the school year
was over. One of her pupils had sung her praises so
much that a friend of his parents had come to see her
at the school to ask if she would give his little daughter
English lessons during the summer vacation. At first
Georgia had been reluctant to give up so much of her
holiday. But in the end the thought of a summer in
Tuscany had been too tempting to pass up and she
accepted, after stipulating that she must spend a week
at home first.

Georgia leaned on the parapet dreamily, her
heartbeat in rhythm with the throb of traffic from the
autostrada across the Arno as she gazed at the view.
Venice had been the realisation of all her dreams of

Italy. But Florence, with its incredible wealth of Renaissance art, promised to surpass them.

Charlotte and Tom were spending a night of luxury here with her at the Lucchesi, then they were off to a Tuscan farmhouse for the rest of their holiday, to laze beside a pool and recharge their batteries before returning to London, where Charlotte, a legal secretary who'd married her boss, worked for her busy solicitor husband.

For Georgia tomorrow would be different. Signor Marco Sardi was sending someone to drive her to the Villa Toscana, where her duties as English teacher to young Alessandra Sardi would begin immediately.

Deciding that a bath was the next thing on the agenda, Georgia moved the flowerpots back in place, then looked up in surprise as Tom's anxious face appeared above the stone partition that divided her balcony from theirs.

'Georgia, come in here a minute, please!'

'Something wrong?'

'Charlotte's not feeling too good.'

Georgia raced next door in alarm.

'What's up?' she said urgently as Tom, wearing a hotel bathrobe only a shade paler than his worried face, let her in.

'She's throwing up in the bathroom,' he said. 'You speak the lingo, Georgie. I think we need a doctor.'

Georgia went into the bathroom where her sister was bent over the basin, sluicing cold water over her face.

'I just lost the cheese rolls,' gasped Charlotte, reaching blindly for a towel. 'Take no notice of Tom— I most definitely don't need a doctor. You know my stomach doesn't travel well. The taxi ride from the station was a bit too exciting for it.'

Georgia put her arms round her sister carefully and held her close. 'You're shivering,' she said sternly.

'You would be too, if you'd just lost the entire contents of your digestive system!'

Georgia led her back into the bedroom to a very worried Tom.

'Darling, I'm all right. Really I am,' said Charlotte as he took her in his arms. 'I just need a shower and some tea and dry biscuits or something. When I'm feeling braver I'll take some of that revolting stomach gloop Mother forced on me.'

'Thank God she did,' said Tom fervently as he drew the sheet over her.

Georgia gave the order to Room Service, made sure that there was nothing more she could do for Charlotte, then went back to her room to shower.

Later, in a brief, almond-pink dress, her heavy, sun-streaked hair framing a glowing, lightly tanned face, she joined Tom and Charlotte to find the latter still in bed, looking pale but less haggard, and triumphant at having retained the tea and toast that Georgia had ordered.

'Oh, Lord, Georgie, you look so *healthy*,' groaned Charlotte.

'And gorgeous to boot,' added Tom, with a leer. 'Now you're here, little sister, I'll take a shower.'

Charlotte eyed him in alarm. 'Darling, shower in Georgie's bathroom, would you? I might need ours in a hurry if I lose the toast.'

Tom Hannay assured his wife that he would do anything in the world for her, collected Georgia's key and took himself next door.

'I'm so sorry, Georgie,' said Charlotte in remorse as her sister perched on the end of the bed. 'I've rather put a damper on things. I can't face the thought of dinner.'

'Of course you can't,' said Georgia cheerfully, and thrust a strand of gleaming hair behind her ear. 'We'll have a meal up here instead.'

Charlotte looked guiltier than ever. 'I can't face the thought of *your* dinner, either. I'd much rather you and Tom went down to the restaurant. I can doze a bit, and you and Tom can enjoy a proper meal.'

'But we can't just leave you here alone!'

'Oh, yes, you can.' Charlotte yawned and slid deeper in the bed. 'To be honest, I quite fancy a couple of hours' rest on my own. I need to recharge my batteries for tomorrow, and the drive through all this Tuscan scenery they rave about.' Her face lit with a smile as Tom came in, rubbing his wet hair with the sleeve of his robe. 'I was just telling Georgia you must both go down to dinner and leave me here for a bit to recover. Then she can order a snack for me when you come up later.'

Tom protested vigorously at first, but Charlotte won him over with the smile he could never resist. 'I hate leaving you alone, darling,' he told her, smoothing back her hair.

She held her face up for his kiss, smiling. 'Don't worry, Hannay, this is the only time in your life I let you dine with a gorgeous blonde!'

Georgia wrinkled her nose in protest. 'Gorgeous I like, but *not* the other bit, please. Just "fair" will do.'

'That's what they said about Helen of Troy—and look at the trouble she caused,' chuckled Tom. 'Anyway, my fair Miss Fleming, give me a minute then we'll go down. I could eat a horse.'

When they arrived in the dining room only two tables were still unoccupied. The maître d'hôtel led them to one near a window, expressed his regret that Signora Hannay would not be dining, provided them with menus, summoned a wine waiter, and left them alone to make their choice.

'Good thing you booked,' said Georgia later as they ate prosciutto with slices of perfect golden melon. She was halfway through grilled salmon served with a separate dish of tiny, buttery vegetables, when Tom let out a smothered chuckle as he poured Chianti Classico into her glass.

'Don't look now, Georgie, but guess who's sitting in state at the back of the room!'

'Who?' she said indistinctly, still too hungry to be curious about anything other than the contents of her plate.

'The chap who held us up on the plane.'

Georgia glanced up sharply, to find a pair of brilliant blue eyes staring into hers. But to her surprise they glittered with a hostility she could recognise right across the dining room.

'He seems very interested in you,' commented Tom, after a swift look. 'Perhaps he remembers you from the plane. Odd, though. Looks a touch unfriendly. Shall I stroll over and ask why he's glaring at you?'

'Certainly not,' snapped Georgia, then smiled in apology. 'Sorry, Tom. Maybe he thinks he knows me. Which he certainly does not.' She went on eating, her appetite unaffected. It would take more than a black look from some self-important stranger to spoil such a delicious meal for her.

'The waiters are pretty attentive—just like the girls on the plane,' observed Tom with interest.

'I wonder who he is?' she said idly, then laid down her fork at last, with a sigh. 'Mmm, wonderful.'

'Pudding?'

She sighed again regretfully. 'I'm tempted—but no, thanks, I won't. Let's get back to Charlotte.'

'Right.' Tom rose to pull out her chair. 'You can order coffee for three with Charlotte's supper.'

Georgia walked ahead of Tom through the dining room, tensing slightly as her path led past the man from the plane. Willing herself to ignore him, to her annoyance she found her eyes drawn like a magnet to his. Stiffening at the unveiled disapproval in the cold blue gaze, she reached for Tom's hand hastily and hurried from the room.

'I wouldn't have caused a scene,' he protested in the lift.

'Just making sure,' she retorted, still smarting from the experience. 'Signor Sardi's paying my bill, remember. I didn't want repairs to broken furniture on it.'

'No chance—the guy's bigger than me.' Tom ushered her out on the second floor. 'I gave him my best legal scowl. Never fails!'

'Oh, let's forget the wretched man,' said Georgia, secretly deeply dismayed by the disturbing little incident. 'I won't drink coffee with you, Tom. I'll just find out what Charlotte wants from Room Service, then I think I'll turn in. I'm tired.'

'Pity you couldn't have had a day's grace before going off to the job.'

'I know. Never mind. I've been waiting to see Michelangelo's *David* all my life. He won't walk out of the Accademia before I get round to him,' said Georgia brightly.

Charlotte was feeling very much better after a nap, and full of enthusiasm for the soup and toasted sandwich that she asked Georgia to order for her. She chuckled when Tom told her that the impressive Italian from the plane had been dining only a few tables away.

'And looking daggers at our Georgie, would you believe?' he added. 'I was all for confronting him, but she dragged me from the dining room in case I made a fuss.'

'Good move,' approved his wife. 'As I remember it, he was rather larger than you, darling.'

'All right, you two,' broke in Georgia, with a yawn. 'If there's nothing more I can do I'm off to bed.'

'Come and have breakfast with us on our balcony,' suggested Charlotte, kissing her goodnight.

Georgia found an envelope on the floor when she went into her room. It contained a terse message in Italian, instructing her to be in the hotel foyer at eleven the following morning, when she would be collected for the drive to the Villa Toscana.

Georgia frowned. The writing was quite unlike that of Marco Sardi, who had written to her twice during the past few weeks, his style infinitely more courteous than the brusque note in her hand. She shrugged and dropped it in a waste bin. Maybe it was a phone message which had lost something in the transcribing.

She filled a glass with mineral water from the small refrigerator, then went out on the balcony to sit for a while at the table there to enjoy the moonlit night before going to bed. She had lied to Tom about being tired. She'd felt a sudden, familiar desire to be alone.

She stared moodily at the improbable golden moon hanging over the Ponte Vecchio. Why had the blue eyes of the unknown Italian held such hostility? Perhaps he was allergic to blondes. Yet the Renaissance Florentine ideal had been fair hair not too different from her own, though with hazel eyes instead of her own uncompromising black. Georgia's eyes were a throwback to a Spanish great-grand-mother, and the contrast with fair, Fleming hair was striking. Normally it appealed to men on sight. But not to the hostile Italian stranger, obviously. Not that it mattered. She was unlikely to meet him again.

She sat looking at the moon until it dipped out of sight beyond the edge of the balcony, then went reluctantly to bed to spend a restless night, her sleep troubled by blue-eyed monsters who stalked her through her dreams.

CHAPTER TWO

NEXT morning the sun woke Georgia early, and she had showered, dressed and packed long before Tom came knocking to announce that breakfast for three was waiting on the balcony next door.

To Georgia's relief she found Charlotte fully recovered and hungry for their breakfast of yoghurt and fresh rolls spread with preserves. When the two coffee-pots had been drained dry Georgia got up to go.

'You've got the phone number of Villa Toscana, so give me a ring before you go back,' she said as she kissed them both goodbye.

'We'll give you a ring tomorrow!' said Charlotte promptly. 'Just to make sure all's well.'

Georgia laughed, hugged her sister once more, then went off to join the luggage that a porter had already taken down to the foyer. No one, she was told pleasantly, had yet arrived to collect her. Georgia went into the big lounge, installed herself in a pink brocade chair alongside a tall palm, took a large pair of sunglasses from her bag and immersed herself in one of the magazines from the glass-topped table beside her. From time to time she glanced up from the latest offerings from the Italian couturiers, but no one seemed to be waiting for her.

She smiled at some of the excesses thought up by the designers, hoping that her own sartorial restraint would meet with Signor Sardi's approval. Georgia had long legs which she knew looked good in the sand-coloured linen trousers she'd finally chosen. With them she wore flat leather shoes the same gleaming chestnut as her large bag and a plain white cotton shirt tucked in neatly. Her hair was caught back at the nape of her neck with a silk scarf striped in shades of brown and gold.

A few moments later Georgia glanced across at the reception desk and stiffened. A familiar figure was talking to one of the receptionists. The hostile Italian himself, she thought angrily, and buried her nose in the magazine, hoping that he'd be well out of the way before she was collected for the trip to Villa Toscana.

'Signorina Fleming?' enquired a startlingly familiar voice, and Georgia looked up from the magazine in surprise. The man from the plane stood looking down at her, dressed in chalk-pale linen trousers of superb cut, and a shirt the exact colour of the unfriendly eyes that she'd found so hard to get out of her mind the night before.

She inclined her head graciously.

'Allow me to introduce myself,' said the man in rapid Italian. 'I am Gianluca Valori.'

The name had a familiar ring to it. Perhaps he was a footballer. He'd certainly announced it in a way which expected recognition. Georgia preserved a dignified silence, raising her eyes to his in mute enquiry through the dark lenses of her glasses.

'I am to drive you to the Villa Toscana, Miss Fleming,' he went on, plainly irritated by her lack of response. 'Marco Sardi is my brother-in-law. If you doubt me, the hotel manager will confirm my identity.'

Her heart sank. 'That won't be necessary, Signor Valori.' Georgia spoke his language fluently enough, but with a slight English accent that she knew most

Italians found charming. This one, it was plain, did not. Nettled by his attitude, she rose to her feet, hefted her bag, and informed her escort that her luggage was waiting near the reception desk.

Gianluca Valori had only to approach, it became obvious, for any hotel staff available to swarm with offers of help, and Georgia's modest amount of luggage was borne off down the white linen runner laid fresh over the red-carpeted front steps each morning. She waited serenely while her escort settled her bill, bade farewells all round, then ushered her outside to the Lungarno della Zecca Vecchia where a long, crouching black panther of a car lay waiting.

Good grief, thought Georgia in alarm as she saw her luggage piled in the back. I'm travelling in *that*?

Her escort installed her in the passenger seat of the sports car with impersonal courtesy, then got behind the wheel and, within minutes, it seemed to Georgia, Florence was left behind and they were hurtling along the A11 *autostrada* at a speed which frightened her silly.

'You are afraid?' asked the driver eventually, glancing at her colourless face.

'Yes,' she said tersely. 'Could you slow down, please? Otherwise I shall be sick.'

He lifted one shoulder and reduced his speed slightly. 'There is no danger, Miss Fleming.' He smiled crookedly, the first sign of warmth that he'd displayed since his frank male interest on the plane. 'I am an experienced driver.'

'So am I,' she returned, her colour restored a little. 'But not at such speed, nor in a car like this.'

He thawed slightly. 'You like the Supremo? It is our finest achievement, I think.'

Georgia's eyes narrowed. Supremo? *Valori*? Of course. The firm of Valori was small, but it manu-factured some of the most luxurious, speedy cars in the world, and the Supremo was the sports car every man dreamed of owning. Valori racing cars were a legend in the world of Grand Prix too...

She bit her lip in sudden dismay, casting a swift, embarrassed glance at her companion's forceful profile. Oh, dear, oh, dear. No wonder his name was familiar. Gianluca Valori had once been one of the most brilliant racing drivers Italy had ever produced. She'd even seen him on television, his teeth a flash of white below the visor of his peaked cap as he sprayed champagne in laughing triumph on the winners' rostrum.

'You feel ill, Miss Fleming?' he enquired, frowning at her.

'No. Thank you.' Just very, very stupid, she thought bitterly.

'We shall be there shortly,' he informed her. 'The villa is near Lucca, a mere thirty minutes from Florence.'

She nodded, tense, certain that the trip took normal drivers twice as long as Gianluca Valori in his Supremo. They bypassed the walled city of Lucca, then turned off at a more leisurely speed onto a narrow road along a valley through undulating hills, where from time to time a stand of cypress pointed dark fingers like exclamation marks on the horizon, calling attention to the unfolding vista. She caught glimpses of beautiful houses on some of the slopes, then a monastery, before the Supremo nosed carefully down a road which was little more than a track.

At the end of it Gianluca manoeuvred the Supremo through gates leading into a beautiful garden ablaze with flowers and tantalising glimpses of white statuary. And at last they drew up in front of a house very different from the daunting Palladian building that Georgia had half expected. The Villa Toscana was relatively small, a perfect example of architecture from the late eighteenth century, with a strong Napoleonic flavour about its hyacinth-blue walls and white-painted shutters.

'We have arrived,' said Signor Valori drily, eyeing her rapt face.

'Yes,' said Georgia hurriedly. 'Yes, of course.' She gave him a smile for the first time, taking off her glasses to see the colours of Villa Toscana in all their glory. She turned back to him, forgetting her animosity for a moment. 'What an exquisite house!'

He stared into her eyes for a few seconds, then lifted a shoulder and looked at the building, his face sombre.

'My sister had faultless taste. She oversaw the restoration of the villa at every stage.'

Georgia's eyes filled with compassion. So Marco Sardi's dead wife had been Gianluca Valori's sister.

Suddenly a small figure in a pink T-shirt and shorts came flying from the house, and Gianluca Valori leapt from the car to sweep the child up into his embrace, kissing her on both cheeks before tossing her up in the air then catching her again and setting her on her feet.

'Come, Alessa,' he said as Georgia got out of the car. 'Welcome Miss Fleming to your home.'

Blue eyes just like her uncle's surveyed Georgia from a small, pale face beneath glossy black hair braided into a thick plait tied with a pink ribbon. 'I don't know how in English, Luca,' she informed her uncle, eyeing Georgia with reserve.

Georgia smiled as Luca Valori explained that Italian would do, since Miss Fleming spoke their language very well.

'So until your lessons begin you may keep to Italian,' he added, smoothing a hand over the dark hair.

'Hello, Alessandra, I'm very happy to meet you,' said Georgia, holding out her hand.

The child took it with a dignity far beyond her years. 'Welcome to Villa Toscana, miss,' she said with touching formality.

'Thank you.'

A young man came to unload the car as Georgia walked with the child and her uncle into a ravishingly beautiful hall. Inlaid wood gleamed on the floor below half-panelled walls lined with green moiré silk. On one of them hung a great gilt mirror which reflected the vivid colours of flowers arranged in brass jardinières on a pair of marble-topped tables.

A smiling woman in a neat cotton dress came to welcome Luca Valori with a flood of voluble Italian so rapid and accented that Georgia was hard put to it to follow it.

'Slowly, Elsa,' he teased. 'Miss Fleming speaks our language well, but she will not understand if you speak like a river in spate!'

The woman laughed, and spoke more slowly, asking if Georgia would like to go to her room before taking coffee or tea in the conservatory.

'I would like to wash very much,' said Georgia gratefully, then turned to Luca Valori. 'Thank you for driving me here.'

He bowed formally. 'I regret I frightened you with my speed.'

'Did you go zoom-zoom, Luca?' demanded Alessa, eyes sparkling.

'I did. But Miss Fleming was frightened, so I could not zoom-zoom all the way. Which is why we took so long to get here,' he added, raising a sardonic eyebrow at Georgia.

'I'm sorry I delayed you. If you're in a hurry to get away I'll say goodbye now,' she added coolly, and held out her hand.

Alessa giggled and nestled close to her tall uncle. 'Luca lives here now—' Her face clouded suddenly and a strong arm drew her close.

Georgia dropped her hand, finding it difficult to hide her dismay.

'I stayed overnight in Florence to get some business done early this morning. And for the privilege of driving you here, of course.' Luca Valori's smile told her that he knew exactly how she felt. 'I was glad to save Marco the trouble of fetching you because he is busy today. Not,' he added softly, 'that a night in Florence is ever a penance. Last night, in particular, was most interesting.'

'Franco has taken your luggage to your room, miss,' said Elsa, to Georgia's relief. 'If you will follow me, please.'

The bedroom allotted to Georgia was on the top floor of the house. She exclaimed in delight when Elsa threw open the door of a room which was on two levels, the first a small sitting room, the second a bedroom reached by a flight of four gleaming mahogany steps. The entire room was papered in a riot of roses with leaves of a rich, vibrant green which was repeated in the plain carpet. Two armchairs upholstered in rose velvet flanked a writing table with a lamp, opposite a pair of white-shuttered windows. On the balustraded upper level a white crocheted spread covered a bed which lay alongside long windows framing yet another breathtaking view.

Elsa turned a small brass knob in one of the rose-covered walls and threw open a door to reveal wardrobe space and shelves, then climbed the steps and opened a second door. 'The bathroom, Miss Fleming,' she announced. 'When you are ready, please come down and I will take you to the conservatory.'

'Thank you,' said Georgia appreciatively, gazing round at her new quarters. 'This is utterly charming. Where does Alessandra sleep?'

'In the room next to yours, miss, and Pina, her nursemaid, in the room at the end.' Elsa went to the door, then turned. 'Everyone calls her Alessa, miss.' She smiled to soften any suggestion of rebuff and went out.

Georgia went to wash, admiring cream marble and gilt fittings. She brushed out her hair, retied it, then paused, frowning at her mirrored face for a moment as she wondered what there was about it to antagonise a complete stranger. She shrugged, added a touch of lipstick, then went down two flights of stairs to the hall to find Elsa, who emerged from the kitchen regions to take her through a formal sitting room where French windows opened into a short, glass-roofed corridor leading to a large conservatory with a more relaxed atmosphere.

Cane furniture was scattered with bright cushions; newspapers and magazines lay on the numerous tables and green plants were everywhere. There were shirred blinds masking part of the windows from the bright noon sunshine, but wide doors stood open to the gardens, where the sound of running water lent an illusion of coolness to the hot July day.

Luca Valori rose as Georgia joined him, but Alessa was nowhere to be seen. Elsa asked if the young lady would like tea, but Georgia requested the strong Italian coffee she'd become addicted to, and Elsa went off to fetch a fresh pot, leaving an awkward silence behind her.

'Please sit down,' said Luca at last.

Georgia chose one of the sofas, and Luca returned to his chair.

'Is your room to your taste?' he asked politely.

'Yes, indeed. It's charming,' Georgia assured him, feeling on safe ground with the subject of interior decorating until she remembered that everything at the Villa Toscana had been chosen by his dead sister. She turned to gaze through the half-veiled windows. 'The garden looks beautiful. Do I hear running water?'

'A trout stream runs through the grounds.' His mouth curled in a wry smile. 'How polite you are, Miss Fleming.'

She gave him a grave, considering look, and decided against an answer. 'Where is Alessa?'

'She is with Pina, the young nursemaid who has been with her since she was born. Alessa will join us for lunch.' He paused, eyeing her soberly. 'You will need patience. I must warn you that she has no wish to learn English. Nor to go to England with her father.'

'Then must she?' Georgia looked at him very directly. 'I know Signor Sardi wants her to learn English prior to a few months in London with him. But must she go with him? Surely Alessa could stay here, with relatives, perhaps, until he gets back?'

Luca Valori's eyes iced over, as though he resented her trespass into his family's concerns. 'Marco's sister would take Alessa willingly, but he cannot bear to be parted from his child for so long. Therefore she must go with him, and go to school in England for a while.' He hesitated. 'Marco thinks it will be good for her. I think so too.'

'I see.' Georgia saw only too clearly. Her job wouldn't be easy. So that she could instil a modicum of English to make life easier for his little daughter in London was why Marco Sardi had engaged her. But he had made it very plain that warmth and sympathy for his child were of far greater importance.

'You like children?' asked Luca, watching her closely.

'Yes. I've always wanted to teach.' Georgia looked up with a smile as Elsa came in bearing a tray. 'Thank you.'

The woman nodded pleasantly, then excused herself to oversee lunch.

Georgia poured strong black coffee from a silver pot into thin, flowered porcelain, handed a cup to Luca Valori, then added sugar and a dash of cream to her own and drank thirstily, making no further attempt at conversation.

'Was your lover sad to part with you?' Luca Valori said abruptly at last, the harsh question startling her so badly that the cup rocked perilously in the saucer.

Georgia laid it carefully on the table beside her then looked up to meet the blue, dissecting gaze head-on. 'Forgive me; I think I misheard you, Signor Valori.'

He lifted one shoulder in the gesture that she was beginning to know. 'I think not. I asked if your lover objected to surrendering you into my care. Are you pretending he doesn't exist? You forget. I saw you with him on the plane, then again at dinner last night. I was surprised when I learned who you were. Marco told me the young lady he had engaged would be free all summer because her fiancé was serving in Cyprus with the British Army. Obviously he arranged some leave.'

Georgia controlled a rush of cold, undiluted rage. 'No, he did not,' she said stonily. 'My companion, both on the plane and at dinner last night, was my sister's husband. They were in the room next to mine.'

Luca Valori stared at her incredulously. 'Is this true?' he demanded.

'Of course it's true!'

His mouth tightened. 'Then I commiserate with the lady—both in her choice of husband, and her sister.' Eyes blazing with distaste, he leapt to his feet and, without a word, strode from the room.

Georgia stared after him, open-mouthed, too astonished for the moment to be angry. At this point Alessa finally put in an appearance, followed by a shy, dark-haired girl, and Georgia was forced to pull herself together.

Alessa marched towards her purposefully, her face screwed up in concentration. 'Miss Fleming, my uncle regrets. He—he—'

'Has urgent business,' prompted the maid lovingly.

Georgia was deeply glad of it, so relieved that her smile was warm enough to dispel the girl's shyness. 'You must be Pina,' she said.

Pina nodded, smiling, then excused herself to go off to the kitchen.

'I wanted Luca to stay to lunch,' said Alessa, pouting, then fixed Georgia with a mutinous blue eye. 'Are you going to start lessons today, miss?'

'No, not today. I thought you might show me round your garden, perhaps your room and your toys too. So no lessons.' Georgia smiled gently at the little girl. 'And my name is Georgia. I prefer that to "miss".'

'Georgia,' repeated Alessa, frowning. 'Is that an English name?'

'I suppose so.' Georgia laughed. 'My father wanted boys, you see, so my sister's name is Charlotte instead of Charles—Carlo to you—and when I arrived I wasn't a boy either, so I am Georgia, instead of George or Giorgio—'

To her horror the small face crumpled and tears streamed down Alessa's face. She knuckled her eyes in misery and Georgia drew the child into a gentle embrace, making soothing, inarticulate noises of comfort until the sobs lessened.

'What is it, darling?' she asked gently. 'Can you tell me?'

'Mamma had—a boy baby—but they both—went to heaven.' Alessa sobbed, rigid and unyielding at first. But at last she abandoned herself to the embrace, seeking comfort like a little animal as she burrowed against Georgia's chest, her tears soaking through the white shirt. Georgia held her tightly, responding fiercely to the child's sorrow.

'Cry, darling,' she said huskily. 'Let it all out.' Secretly she was horrified. Naturally no one had found it necessary to tell her that Maddalena Sardi had died in childbirth, nor, she realised with foreboding, how recently it had happened.

It was a long time before Alessa calmed down sufficiently to detach herself, at which point both of them were very damp and the small face was lobster-pink and swollen.

'I think we'd better change our shirts, Alessa,' said Georgia. 'Shall we find Pina, or can you take me to your room and show me where your clothes are?'

Alessa thought it over at some length, then, with a hiccuping little sob, agreed to take Georgia up to her room. It was charming, painted pink and white, with many educational toys and books, as well as the collection of soft dolls that Alessa showed her visitor with pride.

'My clothes are here,' announced the child, opening a white wardrobe with scenes from fairy tales stencilled on the door. Georgia helped Alessa off with the damp pink T-shirt, replaced it with a clean white one, helped her wash her face in the adjoining pink and white bathroom, then asked her to come next door to her own room.

'You may find a surprise in here,' she told the little girl as they went in.

Alessa's face lit up. 'A surprise for me?'

'No one else!' Georgia opened one of her bags and took out a large, gaily-wrapped box. 'There. All the way from England for Signorina Sardi.'

Alessa knelt on the floor, tearing off the paper to reveal a large cardboard box. She lifted the lid with impatient hands, then put them to her mouth, her eyes saucer-wide with delight. A large, soft doll lay inside, wearing a dress, socks and shoes, her golden hair arranged in two braids which hung to her waist, and tucked in beside her was a small suitcase.

'That's her wardrobe,' said Georgia, changing into a sleeveless blouse. 'You can take her clothes off and dress her in two different sets. Do you like her?'

Alessa nodded vigorously, clapping her hands. 'She is beautiful, miss—Georgia! You brought her all the way from England for me?'

'I certainly did. Shall we take her from the box?' Georgia smiled, relieved. It was pure bribery, of course, to give a six-year-old such an expensive present, but, given the limited time she'd have to get to know Alessa Sardi, it had seemed like a good idea. And the doll had banished all trace of the child's tears. It had been worth it for that alone, thought Georgia with compassion as they went downstairs. Alessa danced ahead to display her present to Elsa and Pina, then ran back to Georgia to say that lunch was ready in the conservatory.

'I shall call her Luisa, and she can have Luca's place,' announced Alessa, and frowned. 'He couldn't stay for lunch, Elsa,' she told the housekeeper as the first course was brought in.

Wouldn't stay, more likely, thought Georgia, condemning Luca Valori out of hand for disappointing his little niece. And if he'd been away why hadn't *he* brought Alessa a gift too?

But as they were beginning on plates of delicious pasta with mushrooms, the first of the ceps, or *porcini*, much prized in Italian cooking, they heard the sound of a car, and minutes later Luca Valori strode into the conservatory, telling his ecstatic niece that he'd changed his mind. Business could wait until tomorrow.

'I decided you were more important than any business,' he told Alessa, then looked across at Georgia, his blue eyes hard. 'I confused what is important and what is not. But only for a while.' Then he applied himself with appetite to the pasta swiftly brought to him, and greeted the chicken *cacciatora* which followed with equal enthusiasm. So did Georgia.

It would take more than Mr Hotshot Valori to put her off her food, she thought, especially when it was of the quality served at the Villa Toscana. And conversation was no problem because Alessa was so thrilled with her English doll that it was the main topic for the meal.

'You are very lucky,' remarked her uncle at one point. 'It is a very beautiful gift.' He smiled at the little girl, his eyes dancing. 'You have not asked me what *I* brought you.'

'Papa says I must not,' said Alessa virtuously, but curiosity overcame her good resolutions. 'What did you bring me, Luca? Is it a doll too?'

'No, it is not, and I think you shall wait until this evening to receive it, now you have such a beautiful gift from Miss Fleming already.'

'Her name is Georgia,' Alessa informed him importantly, and turned enquiringly. 'Shall Luca call you Georgia too?'

'Of course. If he wishes to,' added Georgia serenely, her smile saccharine as she turned it on Luca Valori.

'How kind,' he returned blandly, then turned to Alessa. 'What are you going to do this afternoon, little one?'

'Will you come with me in the pool, Luca?' she pleaded.

He patted her cheek regretfully. 'Alas, I am expecting a very important call from Milan soon. Perhaps later, darling.'

'I could take you in the pool, Alessa,' offered Georgia.

The little girl looked doubtful. The new teacher was obviously no substitute for the glamorous uncle. 'Can you swim, miss—Georgia?'

'I certainly can. Can you?'

Alessa shook her head.

'Then I can start teaching you. This very afternoon, if you like.'

Alessa clapped her hands in glee. 'Oh, *yes*—please,' she added belatedly, and picked up the doll. 'Come, Luisa, we must find Pina and change our clothes.'

As Georgia got up she gave Luca Valori a cool little smile. 'If you'll excuse us, then?'

'No doubt I'll see you later,' he said with rather chilling significance.

Not, she thought drily, if I see you first. But of course that was nonsense. If Luca Valori lived at the Villa Toscana there was no way that she could avoid seeing him.

She sighed. Too bad that the most attractive man she'd met in her entire life thought she was having an affair with her sister's husband. She'd have to put him right on that subject as soon as possible, and not just for her reputation's sake either, she realised, a militant gleam in her eye. Open hostility from any man, whatever his nationality, was a new experience, and surprisingly hard to take. Hurt pride, if nothing else, made it imperative to try and change his mind about her before she left the Villa Toscana.

CHAPTER THREE

THE afternoon was a great help in Georgia's campaign to win the heart of Alessa Sardi. The pool in the gardens was a large, kidney-shaped affair, deep enough at one end for Alessa to be prohibited from the water unless accompanied by an adult.

'So I can only go in the pool with Papa or Luca,' explained Alessa as she slid into the water into Georgia's embrace. She shrieked with delight as Georgia towed her by the hands across the shallow end.

'Now you hold onto the edge of the pool and kick with your legs, then I'll show you how to move both legs *and* arms,' said Georgia, and moved off through the water in the stylish breast-stroke she'd learned at school. 'There,' she said, thrusting her wet hair back as she stood up in the shallow end. 'Now I'll take your chin, Alessa, and you try to copy me. That's right, darling, relax—I shan't let you go.'

With Pina for an admiring audience, the swimming lesson proceeded very successfully, ending in a noisy splashing session and a game with a ball in the shallow end. When Georgia delivered the little girl up into Pina's waiting towel she tensed as she saw a tall, bronzed figure dive cleanly into the water at the far end, and, swimming with a powerful, easy crawl, Luca Valori was on his feet beside her in the shallow end within seconds. He smiled up at his excited little niece, then turned to Georgia.

'You did well, Miss Fleming. I watched the lesson from my bedroom window.'

Georgia, at close quarters to the spectacular body of Luca Valori, forgot any idea of charming him in her hurry to get away. 'Alessa loves the water fortunately. Please excuse me; I must shower and dry my hair.'

For answer he heaved himself up out of the pool in a single movement and leaned down to give her a helping hand. Georgia was forced to take it, and let him pull her from the water, glad that her plain black swimsuit was functional rather than alluring as she hurried to collect her robe and wrap herself in it.

'Pina says we have English tea for you, Georgia,' said Alessa from the folds of her towel as the maid slid sandals onto the child's feet. 'And Elsa has made little cakes.'

'Lovely!' Georgia smiled at her warmly. 'Then I shall hurry through my shower and meet you—where, Alessa?'

'In the garden, if you wish.' Luca Valori waved towards a table and chairs shielded by a large canvas umbrella.

'Alessa shall choose,' said Georgia lightly.

'The garden, the garden,' chanted the child, and smiled pleadingly at her uncle. 'You too, Luca.'

He bowed, laying a hand theatrically on his heart. 'I obey your command, princess.'

She laughed delightedly, then pulled at Georgia's hand. 'Hurry, then. Come *on*, Pina.'

Georgia followed Alessa and Pina upstairs, promising to be down in the garden as soon as her hair was dry. She stood under a hot shower, shampooed her hair and sat looking through the windows at the

Tuscan hills afterwards, frowning as she wielded her hair-dryer. At some stage she would have to take the bull by the horns and ask Luca Valori what she'd done to offend him, why her explanation about Tom had merely made matters worse. He might complain to his brother-in-law. And the last thing she needed was Marco Sardi's disapproval. It wouldn't do her standing at the school in Venice any good if it was known that he'd dispensed with her services.

She grimaced at the thought as she put on a fresh yellow polo shirt with her linen trousers, slid her feet into thonged brown sandals and left her hair loose to finish drying in the afternoon sunshine. She smoothed moisturiser into her flushed face, added a touch of rose-brown lipstick, then went to open the door in answer to a peremptory knock. Alessa was outside, wearing a vividly printed sundress. The dark hair was tied in bunches above her ears, and her blue eyes were sparkling as she clutched the new doll, who was now wearing jeans and a T-shirt.

'Are you ready, Georgia?'

'I certainly am, Miss Sardi. Where's Pina?'

'Gone to tell Elsa we are ready.' Alessa slid a small hand into Georgia's as they went downstairs, chattering about how smart the doll Luisa looked, and how much she'd liked the swimming lesson. 'Can we swim every day?' she asked eagerly.

'Of course—once we've done our English lessons.'

'Oh.' The small mouth drooped.

'They will be fun, I promise,' said Georgia firmly.

In the garden the table was laid ready with a silver tea-service and a coffee-pot, plates of petits fours and almond biscuits. Pina stood hovering, waiting for them, and Luca Valori, now fully dressed, to Georgia's relief, waited to pull out chairs for both ladies, while Pina filled cups and passed plates.

'You enjoyed your swim, Miss Fleming?' enquired Luca, accepting a cup of coffee from Pina.

'Very much. It's a great luxury to have a pool at one's disposal,' she said politely.

'There was no pool at our other house,' said Alessa, drinking milk through a straw.

'The restoration of this house was completed only recently,' explained Luca, his face shadowed.

So Maddalena Sardi had been allowed very little time to enjoy the fruits of her labours.

'I wondered why Alessa couldn't swim,' Georgia said quietly.

'Little one, why not play ball with Pina for a while until Miss Fleming has finished her tea?' suggested Luca, smiling at his niece.

Alessa pouted for a moment, then nodded obediently. 'Will you come too, later?'

'Of course.' He watched as the child scampered away across the grass with Pina, his eyes sombre.

Georgia braced herself. 'Signor Valori, I need to avoid upsetting Alessa in any way. I've no wish to intrude, but would you be kind enough to let me know just a little about her mother, please?'

'Very well.' Luca held out his cup for more coffee. 'Maddalena died six months ago, only a short time after the move to Villa Toscana. She was ten years older than me, you understand, and stronger in mind and personality always than in body. Her physician was deeply concerned when she became pregnant again at the age of forty-three.' He paused, frowning. 'I am sure Marco will not mind my telling you this.'

'Alessa told me she went to heaven with a baby boy,' said Georgia, staring down at her clasped hands. 'It was—heartbreaking.'

'The exact word.' He cleared his throat. 'We were all heartbroken. Marco most of all, naturally. A husband cannot help but feel guilt in such circumstances.' His voice deepened and grew husky. 'My sister was determined to bear a son, but the result was tragedy.'

'I'm deeply sorry—' Georgia's voice failed. Tears stung behind her dark glasses, and she turned away from the surprised blue eyes to look across the garden to where Alessa was chasing a large coloured ball. The silence lengthened, broken only by the laughter of the child as Pina lost the ball in the shrubbery.

'Miss Fleming, I have decided to say nothing to Marco,' said Luca at last.

Georgia looked at him blankly. 'Would he object to my knowing the facts?'

'You mistake me. I meant that I would say nothing on the subject of your brother-in-law.'

She stiffened. 'Signor Valori, there is nothing *to* say on the subject.'

'You will forgive me if I disagree,' he said silkily, then looked up as Franco, the gardener, came to announce that the English lady was wanted on the telephone.

'Speak of the devil,' murmured Georgia, getting up.

Luca followed suit, eyeing her narrowly. 'Devil?'

'Nothing personal,' she assured him. 'Excuse me. Please tell Alessa I won't be long.'

Georgia hurried into the house as fast as her long legs could carry her. Franco showed her into a small study at the back of the hall, then left her to talk in private.

As expected, Charlotte was on the line. 'Hurry up, slowcoach,' said her sister. 'What took you so long? This is costing me money!'

'I was in the gardens. You should see the place, love; it's a gem of a house, with a pool and its very own trout stream!' Georgia went on to astonish her sister with the identity of the man on the plane, described the terrifying drive from Florence to the Villa Toscana with a Formula One ace at the wheel, and, for the crowning touch, related Luca Valori's suspicions about Tom in the role of Georgia's lover.

'But didn't you enlighten him—tell him about James?' demanded Charlotte, when she'd stopped shrieking with laughter.

'Of course I did. But he already knew about James, and for some strange reason the fact that Tom's my brother-in-law seemed to make things worse! Anyway, enough about me. Are you better?'

Charlotte, it seemed, was feeling wonderful, the farmhouse was too romantic for words, Tom was standing at her elbow, demanding to hear the joke, and her phonecard was running out.

'Ring you again next week, before we go back,' said Charlotte, 'and, Georgia, make sure—'

The line went dead and Georgia went back to the garden, feeling suddenly homesick. To her relief only Alessa was waiting for her. Luca Valori was nowhere in sight.

'My uncle has writing to do,' announced the little girl. 'Who was on the phone?' she added inquisitively.

'My sister. She's on holiday here with her husband. Well, not here, exactly, but not very far away. Now, how about a tour of the gardens? You can show me all your favourite places.'

Alessa assented eagerly, proud and happy to show Georgia the trout stream gurgling over the stones in its bed, and the kitchen garden, where all kinds of vegetables thrived under Franco's hand. Great camellia trees and other flowering species strange to Georgia gave pools of shade where a statue stood out palely here and there, and beds full of hydrangeas and geraniums blazed bright in the sunshine.

In the farthest corner of the gardens, out of sight of the house, a neglected old summer house stood high on tall supports, half-hidden among a stand of cypress. Alessa climbed the flight of rather perilous wooden steps eagerly and opened the door to reveal a hot room smelling of sun and dust, with battered wicker furniture and a view of the distant monastery from its windows.

'I love this little house,' said Alessa, throwing herself down on one of the chairs, 'but Papa says I must never come here alone.'

Georgia could see his point. 'We'll come here together. We could even do our lessons here sometimes, if you like.'

Alessa's expressive little face lit up. 'Can we? Papa thought you would want to use his study.'

'If he wants that, then of course we will. But if you'd prefer lessons in your room, or the conservatory, or here, we'll ask his permission, shall we?'

The child expressed delighted approval, to the point of taking Georgia's hand, unasked, as they went down the steps, her new doll clutched firmly in the other. As they went along the gravelled drive to the house Georgia felt that she'd begun to make a reasonable start in winning the child's confidence. And Luca Valori, it seemed, had no intention of running to Marco Sardi with tales behind her back. Big of him, she thought as Alessa chattered like a little monkey. Not that there was anything to tell—something she'd make clear in words of one syllable at the first opportunity.

This came sooner than expected. Marco Sardi would be home late that night, Elsa announced to his daughter's intense disappointment when they got back to the house.

'He will come to see you in bed,' she assured Alessa, then smiled at Georgia. 'He asked me to welcome you to Villa Toscana, miss, and has requested Signor Luca to look after you at dinner. If he is late, he will see you in the morning before he leaves for the day.'

'Thank you, Elsa.' Georgia smiled rather ruefully. A dinner alone with a handsome man like Luca Valori should have been something to look forward to. But, with his disapproval for company, it was likely to be an ordeal. Wondering if she could possibly plead fatigue and ask for a tray in her room, she discarded the idea regretfully. Apparently it was taken for granted that the young English teacher would eat with the family—a privilege she had by no means been sure of. It would be churlish to give Elsa and her cohorts extra work. Besides, Luca Valori would think that she'd lost her bottle.

She grinned as she followed Alessa back to the garden for half an hour before the child's bathtime. None of her friends would ever believe that she'd had dinner with Gianluca Valori, the racing driver who, during his brief, shining hour of glory, had ranked with people like Mansell, Alesi, and the brilliant, doomed Ayrton Senna.

When Alessa pleaded with Georgia to supervise her bathtime, Georgia assented gladly, surprised when in return Pina offered to unpack Georgia's cases and put her clothes away for her.

Georgia agreed, delighted, far happier with a riotous half-hour in Alessa's bathroom than a session of unpacking. After several races with toy boats through the bubbles she helped wash Alessa's thick black hair, then swathed the child in a towel and cuddled her for a while before putting the diminutive nightie on her. Georgia brushed and dried the long, lustrous strands, her heart aching as the little girl leaned against her trustingly. Wealth and luxury were no substitute for a mother. The mere thought of losing her own mother gave Georgia a sharp, physical pain. And she was a grown woman of twenty-six. What it must be like for a child twenty years younger she shuddered to think, and hugged Alessa close.

'I'm sure you can read very well for yourself,' said Georgia diplomatically, 'but because this is our first day together, would you like me to read you a story before you go to bed?'

Alessa, her eyes heavy by this time, agreed readily. Her papa read to her when he came home early enough, she told Georgia, and ran to fetch an Italian translation of collected fairy tales from round the world. Georgia, beginning to feel slightly weary herself after a long day of speaking only Italian, summoned up her best dramatic style as she read *Puss-in-Boots* with a different voice for each character.

When Pina came to see if Alessa was ready for bed, she stayed to listen, her eyes so loving as they rested on the child's face that Georgia felt reassured on one point: Alessa might have lost her mother, but she lacked nothing in the way of love from this girl, not to mention her father, uncle, and the brisk, dependable Elsa.

When the story was over Alessa made no demur when Pina said that it was time for bed. She thanked Georgia without being prompted, asked if she might have another story the following night, and climbed into bed with a sigh.

'I was cross with Papa about the English teacher. But I like you, Georgia. Do you like me?'

Georgia's eyes met Pina's over the glossy dark head, glad to see no hint of jealousy in the maid's indulgent smile. 'I like you very much indeed, Alessa. We shall get on well together.'

The small head nodded, then burrowed deeper into the pillow. 'Goodnight, Georgia.'

'Goodnight, darling. I'll see you in the morning.'

To Georgia's surprise she found her clothes not only unpacked and put away, but any crumpled garments neatly ironed.

'Pina, you're an angel,' she said out loud, and looked through the selection hanging in the wardrobe, wondering what was a suitable choice for dinner with a man who thought she was having an affair with her sister's husband. She grinned, picturing Tom's mirth when Charlotte passed the news on to him, then took down a plain black linen dress and held it against her, eyeing her reflection in the mirror-lined wardrobe. Just the thing. Drop pearl earrings and black linen pumps and she'd be suitably sober.

But dinner wasn't until eight. She would write to James, then read until dinnertime. She ran a gloating eye along the row of books that Pina had unpacked from her holdall. At the school in Venice she taught one-to-one lessons to adults most evenings, and was usually too tired to do anything afterwards except watch television for a bit before falling asleep. Here at the villa she would have a rest after lunch, also this part of the day to herself, and she meant to make good use of both.

The letter to James was oddly difficult. He had disapproved of the vacation job in no uncertain terms in his last letter, which had irritated Georgia, and only spurred her on to accept, which made it a little difficult to describe her present location in the glowing terms it deserved. She bit her lip, trying to conjure up his face, but an ineluctably Latin face with blue, disapproving eyes, kept blotting out James's fair, Anglo-Saxon features. Georgia shooed it away irritably, feeling disloyal.

Not that she was officially engaged to James. She had described him as her fiancé to Marco Sardi mainly because she loathed the term boyfriend. But the fact that she wore no ring yet was her own fault, not James's. Her reluctance to become an army wife was the stumbling block. She wanted a career of her own first, to see some of the world independently. Which James found hard to swallow, but put up with because he was intent on making the army his entire career, and was willing to wait for Georgia until she was ready to settle down with him.

Georgia wrote a cheerful little letter at last, concentrating on the flight and the night in the hotel rather than on the glories of the Villa Toscana, and picked up her book afterwards with a sigh of rather guilty relief.

Georgia curled up in one of the chairs with Wilkie Collins's *Woman in White*, and quickly became so enthralled that she shot out of the chair at last with only fifteen minutes to spare. She had to hurry to achieve an effect so impeccably restrained that Luca Valori would be forced to change his mind about her.

At eight precisely Georgia was ready. Perfumed and made up with great care—just the right dramatic emphasis for the eyes which looked so striking against the heavy, ash-fair hair she caught back with a black velvet ribbon. Other than her gold watch, the heavy *faux* pearl drops were her only ornament, and she eyed herself critically, feeling pleased with the result.

Like a general going into battle she descended the stairs, ready to take on the enemy, who appeared in the hall, right on cue, just as she reached it. Luca Valori was dressed in very much the same way as he had been in the morning, except that, tonight, shoes and trousers were black. The shirt, however, was the same shade of blue. Georgia smiled politely, wondering scornfully if he had all his shirts made for him in that precise shade to match his eyes. Poser!

'You look very elegant this evening, Miss Fleming.' He ushered her into the small, formal drawing room, where a tray of canapés and drinks waited on one of the marble-topped tables.

'Thank you,' she returned with composure.

He gestured towards the silver tray of bottles. 'What would you like?'

'Tonic water, please.'

His eyebrows rose. 'Can I not tempt you to an aperitif?'

'No, thank you. I rarely drink—other than a glass of wine with dinner.'

He shrugged. 'Then tonic water you must have.'

'Thank you.' Georgia accepted the drink and sat down, making no attempt at conversation.

'Are you always as silent?' he enquired at last, then smiled slowly. 'But of course you are not. I had evidence of that last night. With the fortunate brother-in-law you were very animated.'

'I've known Tom a long time.' She looked at him expressionlessly as he seated himself on the other side of the table.

'Evidently. But is your sister aware that your relationship with him is so very—*intimate*?' Luca gave her a caustic look, then drank half the glass of wine he'd poured for himself.

The open implication in his tone put paid to any explanations. Georgia seethed in silence, abandoning her plan to win Luca Valori round. Why should she justify her behaviour to a complete stranger? If Marco Sardi required enlightenment, fair enough. He was not only paying her wages, but was a kind, fatherly man whom she very much respected, from her short acquaintance with him. But Luca Valori, other than by his relationship with Alessa, had no right of any kind to sit in judgement.

She finished her drink and got to her feet briskly. 'Signor Valori, I'm sure you'll be relieved if I take myself off to my room rather than inflict my company on you at dinner. Perhaps you'd ask Elsa to send something to my room on a tray?'

Luca leapt to his feet, a hand out towards her in apology, then swung round in surprise as a quiet voice from the doorway said, 'I trust that will not be necessary, now I am here, Miss Fleming.'

Both protagonists turned sharply to confront the dark, tired man who stood watching them, one eyebrow raised.

'Marco! You are early,' exclaimed Luca with a smile, in no way discomfited by the arrival of his dead sister's husband—unlike Georgia, who blushed vividly in embarrassment.

Marco Sardi took her hand, looking amused. 'How do you do, Miss Fleming? I *had* hoped you were being treated well in my absence.'

Luca shrugged gracefully. 'A slight misunderstanding only, Marco.'

'I rejoice to hear it, Luca. Miss Fleming is our guest, and comes to us with the highest recommendations. It would be a great pity if she felt it necessary to catch the next flight from Pisa back to London.'

Georgia gazed at the drawn, clever face of Marco Sardi with gratitude. 'Ah, but I've made Alessa's acquaintance already, Signor Sardi. She is enchanting. Unless *you* ask me to go, I'd very much like to stay.'

'Good. I am most relieved.' His dark eyes rested on one face then the other. 'Please look after our guest, Luca, while I visit my daughter. Give me a few minutes to bathe before dinner and I will join you as swiftly as I can.'

Luca Valori smiled in reassurance at his brother-in-law, then turned with deliberate formality to Georgia. 'Miss Fleming, forgive me, I beg, or Marco will make my life hideous—Alessa also.'

Georgia inclined her head, deliberately gracious.

Marco Sardi looked from one to the other with an approving smile. 'Now, if you will excuse me, I shall be as swift as possible. I shall apologise to Elsa on my way for holding up dinner.'

CHAPTER FOUR

THE dining room at the Villa Toscana was used only for the most formal of meals, Georgia learned. Family dinner, just like lunch, was served in the conservatory. With an almost full moon lighting up the garden the view through the open doors was breathtaking and Luca Valori, to Georgia's surprise, suggested that she might care to stroll outside until Marco joined them.

She agreed cautiously. A walk across moonlit lawns was better than sitting inside together in fraught silence. And at first the silence continued as they walked, Georgia determined that Luca should be the first to break it.

'I wish,' he said at last, the deep, gravel-toned timbre of his voice more accentuated than usual, 'that I could turn the clock back to my first sight of you on the plane.'

'Oh?' said Georgia without encouragement.

He gave her a morose, sidelong look as they paced slowly. 'Before I realised you were not alone. That you were with a man.' He lifted a shoulder. 'How could you not be?'

'What does that mean?' she demanded hotly.

'You are very beautiful—I meant nothing more than that,' he said, equally heated.

'Oh.' Georgia subsided. No one had ever called her beautiful before. Not even James. Attractive, even striking sometimes, but not beautiful. Maybe the word gained something in translation.

'Do you intend to marry your fiancé soon?' he asked after a while, apparently forgetting about intrusion in her private concerns.

Georgia's instinct was to tell him to mind his own business, but, to keep the peace, she shook her head. 'No. We're in no hurry.' At least, I'm not, she amended silently. 'James is doing his six-month *roulement* in Cyprus with the British Army. From his letters it sounds like a lot of fun. James plays polo rather a lot.'

'Will you enjoy being a soldier's wife?'

'Probably.'

'You display little enthusiasm.' He gave her a brooding look as they strolled along the banks of the stream.

'James is a career soldier. In other words, the army is his life. I want to go on with my own career for a year or two before I turn into an army wife.'

Luca Valori gave his one-shouldered shrug. 'Or is the true reason a little different? Because the man you truly want is married already?'

Georgia's hands clenched into fists. 'Signor Valori, I am trying hard not to lose my temper. But can't you take my word for it that you're mistaken about my relationship with Tom?'

'As was agreed before,' he returned coldly, 'it is not my concern.'

She breathed in deeply. 'Right. Let's talk about something else—politics, religion, football; anything other than my love life!'

Luca stopped, and looked down into her upturned face, his eyes unfathomable in the moonlight.

'Perhaps we should begin again, erase everything before this moment in time.'

Georgia stood very still, hypnotised by the look in his heavy-lidded eyes, which were as dark as her own in the uncompromising black and white of the night. She blinked at last, and turned away, groping for the correct words with unaccustomed difficulty, and in the end lapsed into English to make her meaning clear. 'If you mean that for the short time I am here we can achieve some kind of—of civility, then yes, I agree.'

'*Civiltà*!' He gave an odd, brusque laugh. 'How very British!'

They walked in silence for a moment, then he gave her a wry, sidelong glance. 'But what I meant, Miss Georgia Fleming, was that we should continue our acquaintance rather more cordially. Come.' He turned, beckoning her towards the house. 'I suddenly have a great desire for my dinner.'

'So have I. My appetite is a family legend.'

'Good. I like to see a woman eat.'

'Your cuisine here is magical,' said Georgia, in an attempt at lightness. 'I've eaten everything put in front of me the entire year I've worked in Italy, yet I've lost weight!'

Luca laughed. 'I doubt that it is the same for everyone. Perhaps you work too hard.'

'They don't give me my money for nothing at the school,' agreed Georgia, warming to her attempt at friendliness. 'I was quite tired at the end of the academic year. To be honest, instead of coming here to teach Alessa, I wanted to stay home for a while with my parents.'

'Then why did you agree?'

'Signor Sardi's description of Alessa touched me, I suppose.' She smiled ruefully. 'I thought I might be able to help.'

'You were right—Georgia. Now that I am committed to this civility of yours, you permit my use of your name?'

'Yes.'

'You know my name is Luca.' He held out his hand.

Georgia hesitated, then put her hand in his, and he clasped it tightly, looking down at her in a way that made her uneasy, wondering if somewhere, somehow, she'd done something rash. She smiled, detached her hand, then went in to find Marco Sardi waiting at the table.

'Good,' he said with satisfaction, looking from one to the other. 'You have called a truce, I see. Now, let us apply ourselves to Elsa's miraculous cooking. It is a long time since lunch.'

Georgia found, to her relief, that dinner at the Villa Toscana was a surprisingly entertaining experience. In company with two cultured, intelligent men who drew her into the conversation on all topics, her attitude towards Luca Valori gradually changed. Both men were surprised when she said at one point that it was deeply refreshing to have her views consulted about matters some men thought totally beyond her grasp.

'But why?' said Marco Sardi, mystified.

'Because some men would not dream that intelligence lay behind such a face, I think,' said Luca, surprising her with his insight.

'But beauty such as Georgia's is only possible when intelligence illuminates it,' said Marco, then smiled kindly. 'We are making our guest blush.'

But she wasn't really a guest, thought Georgia, merely someone he was paying to teach his daughter. Marco Sardi was a very courteous man.

'But then, Marco, you are used to the combination of brains and beauty,' Luca pointed out. 'Maddalena possessed both in abundance.'

Marco's face looked suddenly haggard. 'Very true. I miss her at the *fabbrica* as much as I miss her in every other way. Without you this past week, Luca, I have been hard pressed.'

'My sister and Marco handled the finances and sales of Fabbrica Valori together,' explained Luca. 'I am interested more in design and the mechanical side, but Marco is ruthless. He insists on sending me off on public-relations exercises. I was returning from one on the flight to Pisa.'

'His name and face sell more cars than any other sales promotion we can devise,' said Marco, making an obvious effort to throw off his melancholy. He looked at Georgia in enquiry. 'I assume you know Luca was expected to be world champion at one time?'

'No, I didn't know that,' said Georgia honestly. 'My father follows the sport avidly, but I'm not much of a Grand Prix fan myself. Though I remember seeing you on TV once, on the rostrum with the usual champagne bottle,' she added to Luca.

'That was before I yielded to Maddalena's urgings and retired to spend more time with the company.' Luca's face was sober. 'After the madness of the eighties, when the demand for our cars was so high that we had problems in meeting it, world recession

hit our industry hard. We have always made luxury
cars, you understand—sports models with style, built
with loving care rather than by the robots of mass
production.'

Marco leaned across and poured a little cognac into
Luca's glass. 'But we weathered the storm, and others
were rescued. Your British Aston Martin Lagonda,
Georgia, was bought up by Ford, and Bugatti are now
restoring Lotus fortunes, but the new Valori Supremo
is outstripping all its rivals.' He laughed. 'Did you
enjoy your ride in it with Luca?'

'Not a lot,' she confessed honestly. 'It was at that
point I realised who he was. I was terrified!'

There was general laughter, then Luca lifted a
shoulder in the now familiar gesture. 'My passenger's
beautiful face turned green!'

At which Georgia's face turned pink. She got up,
bringing both men to their feet with her. 'I think it's
time I went to bed. You must both have a lot to
discuss, and I must be bright and early for Alessa tomorrow. Perhaps you could give me your instructions
about her lessons in the morning, Signor Sardi?'

'Of course, my dear.' He smiled at her kindly. 'I'm
sure you will be good for my daughter. I need not tell
you how much she means to me. I am selfish to insist
on taking her to England with me, but I am required
there when our London office opens, and must remain
there until all is running smoothly.' His mouth twisted.
'I could not bear to be parted from her that long.
Also Luca agrees with me, that the change of scene
for a while will be good for both Alessa and myself.'

'I can understand that,' said Georgia
with sympathy.

'At the moment Alessa is clinging to everything familiar,' said Luca.

'Which is why Luca is living here. She adores him,' said Marco simply, 'which is also part of the problem about England. She wants Luca to go too, and of course he is needed here.'

'I'll do my best to paint my homeland in glowing colours so she'll look forward to seeing it,' promised Georgia, then smiled at both men. 'Goodnight.'

'Goodnight, Georgia,' said Marco. 'Welcome to Villa Toscana. I hope you enjoy your stay here.'

'I'm sure I will. And I shall try hard to see Alessa enjoys my stay too.'

'I will see you to your room,' said Luca, and, afraid to wreck the fragile peace between them, Georgia made no protest. She walked with him through the drawing room and the dimly lit hall, making a note of the light switches he showed her on the way up both flights of stairs to her door.

'Thank you. Goodnight,' she said as they came to a halt.

'I came to learn whether you spoke the truth,' he said abruptly, and she stiffened.

'About *Tom*?'

He shook his glossy dark head impatiently. 'No! I refuse to discuss your sister's husband further.' He stopped dead, swallowed, then said gruffly, 'I mean your intention to keep to the truce between us. To observe these *civilities* of yours.'

She eyed him militantly. 'I rarely say things I don't mean. Contrary to your impression of me, I'm a pretty straightforward sort of person. The truce won't be broken by *me*—if only for Alessa's sake.'

Luca smiled. And Georgia was glad that she'd told him about James. When Luca Valori chose to exert it his charm was formidable. A fiancé in the background was an effective shield against it. 'Good,' he said softly. 'Life at the Villa Toscana will be more comfortable that way. For all of us.' He raised a slim black eyebrow. 'When you looked at me on the plane I thought you recognised me.'

'Your face was familiar,' Georgia admitted, then gave him a mischievous smile. 'I thought you were a movie star.'

Luca's wide, classically cut mouth twisted in mock disgust. 'No. Nothing so pretty. I like grease on my hands.'

'Were you sorry to give up racing?' she asked curiously.

He nodded. 'Yes, very much. I would lie if I denied it. But then when Ayrton Senna was killed I was devastated—glad I had left the world of the track behind. No one, I realised, is invincible.' He shrugged. 'Valori no longer build Formula-One cars for the Grand Prix circuit. We concentrate now on fast cars for the connoisseur.'

'Your family must be glad.'

His face shadowed. 'It pleased Maddalena. So that, at least, I was able to do for her before she died.'

Impulsively Georgia reached out a hand to him, and he took it. 'I—I'd better say goodnight and get my beauty sleep—' She stopped, biting her lip.

'You have no need of it,' he assured her promptly, and Georgia withdrew her hand, but Luca recaptured it, smiling. 'I think you are not accustomed to hearing your looks described so. Have you heard of Andrea della Robbia?'

She nodded. 'He was a sculptor during the Renaissance.'

'You could have been the model for some of his faces.'

'Then I'll have to go and look at his work, if only out of curiosity!'

'I am willing to be your guide, whenever you wish— if such a thing is allowed within the terms of this truce?'

'That depends on how much time off Signor Sardi allows me,' she said breathlessly. 'Goodnight.'

He reached for her hand, raised it to his lips and kissed it. 'Goodnight, Georgia.' He held onto the hand, his grasp tightening as he straightened to look down into her wary eyes. He moved closer involuntarily, his gaze falling to her mouth, and her heart gave a thump. Then her hand was free and she turned away swiftly into the safety of her room.

Georgia slept better than expected, all things considered, but woke early to keep her rendezvous with Marco Sardi at breakfast in the conservatory. The day was already hot, and the sunshine so bright that she discarded jeans in favour of a dress in thin black cotton dotted with yellow and white.

'Good morning,' said her employer, getting up at her approach. 'You look as though you slept well.'

'I did, indeed. Good morning, Signor Sardi.' Georgia sat down next to him, helping herself to coffee as he indicated. 'I heard Alessa go downstairs with Pina. Where is she?'

'Luca took her into the garden so that we might discuss her lessons in peace.' Marco Sardi held out his cup for more coffee. 'Naturally I will not presume

to instruct you on your method of teaching, only to
ask that you do not work her too hard, and give her
a long rest after lunch. Alessa was far from pleased
at the idea of more lessons now school is over for the
summer.'

Georgia smiled. 'Understandable! But don't worry,
Signor Sardi. The lessons will be short at first, and
as much fun as possible, I promise.'

'Fun,' he repeated, with a wry smile. 'None of my
teachers ever made lessons fun, as I remember. My
friends, the Donatis in Venice, are deeply impressed
by their son's progress in English now he is your pupil.
But, far more important than that to me, they said
you were kind, and loved children.'

'I shall try to be Alessa's friend as well as teacher,'
promised Georgia quickly. 'A very easy task—she's
an endearing child.'

'And the image of her mother.' He rose with a sigh,
his face set in weary lines. 'And now I must leave.
Thank you for rising so early for our talk, Georgia.
You shall report on Alessa's progress at dinner
tonight.'

'Papa, Papa,' called Alessa, running in from the
garden. 'Look what Luca brought me from London!'

'Say good morning to Georgia,' admonished her
father.

Alessa obeyed hastily, with a quick smile for
Georgia, then thrust out her wrist, which was adorned
by a small white watch with large numerals in lu-
minous colours. Marco Sardi admired it with the
requisite extravagance, caught his little daughter up
in a hug and kissed her on both cheeks, then set her
down as Luca, in a superb, handmade grey suit and
the inevitable blue shirt, came strolling in.

'Good morning, Georgia,' he said, with a smile. 'You slept well?'

She returned the smile with reserve. 'Good morning. I slept very well, thank you.'

'Come, Luca, we must be at Valorino by nine,' said Marco.

'But first,' said Luca, 'have you arranged time off for Georgia?'

Marco Sardi clapped a hand to his forehead. 'No, I have not!' He turned to Georgia in apology. 'Weekends are yours, unless some crisis occurs at the *fabbrica*. If I am called away we shall come to some other arrangement.'

Georgia assured him that for the short time she would spend at the Villa Toscana she was quite willing to forgo any time off until the end of her stay. 'I thought I'd spend a short break in Florence afterwards before term starts in Venice.'

'You must have *some* time for yourself,' said Luca emphatically, then glanced at his watch. 'But we can discuss that this evening. Come, Marco, let me drive you—'

'No!' said his brother-in-law, completely without malice. 'We shall go separately, as always. A waste of petrol, but kinder to my nerves.'

When they had gone Alessa looked forlorn for a moment, until asked to share Georgia's breakfast.

'I shall ask Pina to bring more juice and coffee,' she said importantly, very much lady of the house, and soon they were eating fresh hot rolls spread with butter and preserves, washed down with fresh orange juice and strong black coffee diluted, for Alessa, with a great deal of hot milk.

'Good,' said Pina, when she came to clear away. 'You have eaten well today, Alessa.'

The child looked surprised, as though she hadn't noticed how much she'd eaten, then asked Georgia when they could go swimming again.

'After our morning lesson,' said Georgia firmly, steeling herself against the entreaty in the gentian-blue gaze.

'I thought we would start tomorrow,' said Alessa hopefully.

'Your papa wants you to start today,' said Georgia, taking the coward's way out. 'So after breakfast we'll do some lessons. Afterwards we'll go for a walk in the garden, and after that we'll have a swim before lunch.'

Alessa, as Georgia fully expected, proved to be a bright pupil. And, because Georgia produced several visual aids in the shape of photographs and her own brightly coloured drawings, Alessa enjoyed her first lesson. In a surprisingly short time she knew numbers and letters, and could introduce herself in English and say a short phrase or two. She was astonished when Georgia said that it was time to finish.

'Already? Can I speak Italian now?' she demanded as Georgia put her things away.

'Yes, of course. But English only during lessons, Signorina Sardi.'

The rest of the morning passed quickly. During the walk through the gardens, Alessa, intoxicated with her new expertise, demanded the names of the flowers and trees in English. 'I hope Papa comes home early tonight,' she said, skipping along. 'I shall talk to him in English, Georgia. He will be *very* pleased.'

Georgia, secretly very relieved that the lesson had gone so well, agreed that Alessa's papa would be delighted.

'Luca too,' said the child with satisfaction, and held out her wrist to admire the watch. 'Anna and Chiara will be jealous.'

'Who are they?' enquired Georgia as they went indoors to change for swimming.

'My friends at school. They have uncles too, but not famous like Luca.' Alessa scampered off to the beckoning Pina, and Georgia went into her room with a wry smile. Luca Valori obviously gave reflected glory to his little niece.

There were no more lessons that day, other than a reprise of Alessa's new English vocabulary at bathtime. Pina listened with admiration as she bathed and dried her charge, while Georgia sat on a stool, prompting when Alessa faltered.

Afterwards Georgia read another fairy story, but this time Marco Sardi arrived before she'd finished, and Alessa hurled herself into her father's arms, smiled up into his loving face, and said very slowly in English, 'Good evening, Papa; how are you today?'

CHAPTER FIVE

THE pattern of the first day was repeated in almost every detail as others succeeded it. The weather was consistently hot and sunny, and each morning the English lesson was followed by a walk and then a swim, a long rest after lunch, then a game with a ball in the garden while Alessa recapped on the vocabulary she'd learned earlier. And each evening Marco Sardi and Luca Valori were regaled with Alessa's latest English conversation before Georgia went to her room to enjoy a breathing space before joining the men for dinner.

This, she acknowledged to herself as she dressed, was the best part of the day. She was rapidly growing deeply attached to Alessa, but the concentrated one-on-one style of teaching was surprisingly tiring, even with a long break in the middle of the day. Especially when she knew Marco Sardi wanted his daughter capable of the basic necessities in English by the time she left. After Alessa went to bed each evening Georgia was very grateful for the hour or two's grace before dinner, knowing that her work for the day was over.

And, she admitted secretly, each evening at dinner there was Luca Valori for company. Marco Sardi, who missed very little, Georgia knew, behaved as though he was entirely unaware of Luca's growing—and very open—predilection for their 'English guest', as he unfailingly referred to Georgia. As the days went by Luca made it plain that his earlier hostility to Georgia was a thing of the past, that he enjoyed her company, and was strongly attracted to her. Georgia was disturbed by the confidence in his blue eyes, as though Luca Valori had no doubt that she reciprocated whatever it was he felt.

Before coming to Italy, she had been assured by her principal that for a sensible young woman there would be admiration, but little danger from the Italian male of the species. And she had been right. Georgia's looks attracted admiration, but her dealings with Italian men had been mainly with very much married mature professional men, who needed English lessons for their work, or teenage male students who were appreciative but respectful, and never gave her cause for offence.

Luca Valori was something else entirely. For one thing, although their exchanges were always conducted in his own tongue, Georgia knew that he spoke English very well. Life on the international circuit of the racing track would have added to the English he'd probably learned at school, but for some reason he never made any attempt to speak to her in anything but his native tongue. Neither did Marco Sardi, though he, she knew very well, spoke fluent, Tuscan-flavoured English, since their first communications had all been made in her own language.

English was something kept solely for her lessons with Alessa. And Georgia knew that her command of Italian wasn't sufficient to ask Luca if he was just flirting with her, or whether—James or no James— he intended an all-out assault on her defences at some stage. In the light of his suspicions about Tom he might well consider her an easy target, even take it for granted that she'd accept him as a lover. She felt the blood rush to her face at the mere idea.

'You are tired this evening?' asked Marco Sardi as they lingered over coffee.

Georgia smiled, and shook her head. 'Not really. I wish all my pupils were as bright as Alessa.'

Luca turned his lambent blue gaze on her, his eyes moving over each feature of her face with an indolent relish that heightened the colour in her cheeks. 'You find the heat trying, Georgia?' he asked, her name sounding like a caress in the deep, husky voice.

'No,' she said briskly. 'I love the sun.'

'Which is evident. You glow!' He turned sharply at a slight sound from the man beside him. 'What is it, Marco?'

Marco breathed in carefully. 'Nothing,' he said, shrugging. 'I should eat less red meat. It gives me indigestion.'

'If anyone looks tired, Marco, it is you,' said Luca sternly. 'Take the day off tomorrow.'

'No, no,' protested the other man. 'I just need rest.' He rose to his feet, with a smile for Georgia. 'I shall submit to the weakness of age and indulge myself with an early night.'

'Goodnight.' Her smile was sympathetic. 'I hope you feel better by morning.'

'I feel better already,' he assured her, and smiled into Luca's searching eyes. 'Don't worry; I'll be up bright and early tomorrow.'

When he had gone Luca sat in the chair nearest to Georgia's sofa, staring out at the moonlit garden. 'Marco worries me,' he said, frowning.

'I can see that. Is he always so thin?'

'No. He is not. I shall persuade him to visit a doctor. He has been working too hard since Maddalena died.' He lifted a shoulder. 'I understand why. He loved her very much. Theirs was a very passionate marriage, you understand. It is very hard for him in many ways without her.'

Georgia coloured as it dawned on her what he meant.

'I have embarrassed you,' said Luca, looking at her sharply. 'It was not my intention.'

'No, of course not.' She gave him a crooked little smile. 'Sometimes, when I'm tired, my brain slows down and it takes me longer to understand what's said to me. At the school there are other people who speak English. Here I function in Italian all day long, other than the lessons with Alessa.'

'I speak English,' he said abruptly. 'But not as well as you speak Italian, Georgia. And I prefer to talk with you in my own language because your accent charms me. And not only your accent. As you know well,' he added with emphasis.

Georgia rose to her feet precipitately. 'It's time I said goodnight.'

Luca got up more slowly, his eyes holding hers. 'Why? Are you afraid?'

'Not afraid exactly.' She held his gaze unwaveringly as she searched for the right word. 'Prudent? No, wary. That's it. I'm wary,' she went on slowly, digging deep into her vocabulary, 'of giving you, or anyone else, the wrong impression.'

Luca moved closer, the heavy lids veiling the gleam in his eyes. 'Are you saying that because of this soldier of yours you are immune to me? Or is Tom Hannay the real obstacle?'

Georgia's eyes flashed dark, resentful fire at him. 'Will you stop all this nonsense about Tom?'

'I know very well that it is not nonsense at all,' he assured her, in a way that set her teeth on edge. 'I also know I have the power to make you forget him. And all other men—this James of yours included.' And with a sudden movement he caught her in his arms and held her close, the thudding of his heart like a hammer against her breasts. 'Tell me you are indifferent to me—if you can!'

Georgia was quite unable to say anything, struck dumb from the mere fact of being in Luca Valori's arms and wanting so much to be kissed that she couldn't find any words at all, Italian or English.

Luca gave a smothered, exultant laugh and bent his head with tantalising slowness. She was trembling when his mouth met hers at last, with practised enticement. At the contact her lips parted involuntarily and Luca's polished skill vanished. Abruptly they were two breathless, vibrating bodies fired with the same elemental need which surged through them both like an electric current, welding them together with its heat.

For the first time in her life Georgia felt every last scrap of reserve melt in the crucible of the sudden, overwhelming passion which obliterated everything else in the world until the shrill demand of the telephone broke the spell. Luca cursed wildly, and let her go, and Georgia returned to earth with a jolt, breathless and shaken and utterly astounded by the cataclysm that had overtaken her.

Luca snatched up his mobile phone from a nearby table and yanked out the aerial with a force which threatened to break it. 'Valori,' he snarled, listened for a moment, then his face suddenly set into grim, granite lines. To Georgia's surprise he spoke in husky, accented English.

'Of course. I will call her. A moment please.' He almost flung the instrument at Georgia. 'For you,' he snapped, and strode out into the moonlit garden.

Heaving in a deep, ragged breath, Georgia said 'hello' in a voice she hardly recognised as her own.

'Georgia? Is that you? Hi, gorgeous, it's Tom. Was that the hostile Italian?'

'Yes,' she said, resigned, and sat down in the nearest chair abruptly. 'It certainly was. How's Charlotte?'

'Right here at my elbow, panting to talk to you.'

'Out of the way, Tom,' said his wife impatiently. 'Georgie?'

'Hello, Charlotte.'

'Are you OK? You sound odd.'

'Couldn't be better,' lied Georgia. 'Have you stopped being sick?'

'Yes. And now I'm all tanned and brown like you, and blend in with the locals rather well. We actually stirred ourselves to go somewhere yesterday and took a drive to Siena. What a miraculous place! Tom climbed that tower and got dizzy with the view, but I chickened out. Have you had any time off yet?'

'No. I stayed here over last weekend because both Alessa's father and uncle were tied up in work with some crisis. But next weekend I hope to get to Florence.' Georgia listened to her sister enthusing over the marvels of Michelangelo's *David*, promised to queue for hours if necessary to get in to the Accademia to see him, then spoke swiftly, giving her sister messages for their parents before Charlotte's phonecard ran out.

Georgia pressed the off button, thrust the aerial home and put the phone back on the table, then hurried to the door. But her plan to escape Luca failed. He came racing from the garden to intercept her.

'Georgia!'

She turned reluctantly, her eyes questioning on his taut, unsmiling face.

'I ask your forgiveness,' he said harshly. 'It was not my intention to—to behave in such a way.'

Georgia felt suddenly very, very tired.

'You have nothing to say?' he demanded, coming closer.

'I'm too tired to speak Italian,' she said wearily in English. 'So I'll just say goodnight.'

'Please,' he replied in the same tongue. 'First you must understand I did not—did not wish to assault you.'

'I know that,' she said, surprised. 'It was hardly an assault.'

'Perhaps I do not use the right word,' he said, scowling.

'You just wanted to show me how irresistible you can be,' she said, without emotion, and smoothed back hair that had suffered considerably from his attentions.

He stood very erect. 'I wished to show you it is possible to—to make love with other men.'

'*Other* men?' she said, incensed.

'*Dio*! I meant,' he said in exasperation, 'a man who was not this Tom Hannay—nor this fiancé of yours.'

'His name is James. And before I get thoroughly offended I think we'd better revert to Italian,' said Georgia rapidly. 'So you can understand once and for all that to me Tom is just my sister's husband. I'm fond of him, but nothing more. James is—is the man I'm in love with,' she finished in a rush, appalled to find that she was lying.

'I do not believe you,' he said flatly.

Georgia's eyes flashed. 'Whether you believe me or not is irrelevant. Signor Sardi's opinion is the one that counts.'

Luca stared at her implacably. 'You think he would not mind if he knew the truth about your affair with your sister's husband?'

'There is no affair. But tell him if you like,' she said flatly, and turned on her heel, only to find her wrist caught in a grip that bruised as he swung her round to face him.

'And did you tell Tom Hannay that his call came at a most inconsiderate moment?' he demanded, his eyes blazing.

Georgia stared at him. '*Sconsiderato*?' she repeated blankly.

'The wrong moment, then,' he said impatiently, and seized her other hand. 'To feel such joy, such passion, then to be hurled to earth by the sound of the man's voice—' He gave his familiar, eloquent shrug, then pulled her against him, but Georgia stood rigid in his embrace.

'So this is also the wrong moment,' he said bitterly, and thrust her away.

Georgia glared at him. 'For a long list of reasons, there isn't going to be a right moment.'

'Why not?' he said imperiously. 'Can you deny that you responded to me, that you caught fire in my arms?'

'No. And I've no intention of losing my head in that way again. I'm here as an employee, paid to teach

Alessa, so what happened was neither wise nor sensible. And last, but not least, you won't believe me about Tom.' Her voice cracked. 'He's my sister's husband, for pity's sake! I object to your insinuations. Strongly. James would too.'

She glared at him, hoping that he couldn't tell her palms were wet and her mouth dry with the effort it was taking to convince him that he had no hope of breaching her defences again. 'Goodnight,' she said at last, and turned away, half hoping, half dreading that he would leap after her and take her in his arms. But Luca Valori stayed where he was, scowling, and Georgia walked from the room, her head high.

Next morning Marco Sardi was alone in the conservatory when Georgia and Alessa joined him for breakfast.

'Two letters for you, Georgia. Luca brought them in before he left. He wished to oversee some modification they are making to the new Supremo engine,' said Marco, and smiled at his daughter as she tucked into her breakfast. 'You are eating well, my darling,' he said lovingly.

Which was more than could be said for her father, thought Georgia with concern. She had little appetite herself this morning, but that would soon pass. It would take more than a quarrel with Luca Valori to put her off her food for long. But Marco Sardi had been eating very little for days, unless he consumed an enormous meal at some point during his working day. He was growing visibly thinner, and Georgia was uneasy about the greyish tinge to his face. Unable to ask personal questions, she asked instead whether he would be home over the weekend.

'I will indeed,' he said emphatically. 'You have been here nearly two weeks, and so far you have had little time to yourself. Tomorrow is Saturday, and I shall take Alessa to spend the day with my sister and her family. Would you care to come with us? Or perhaps you could come as far as Lucca and do some exploring on your own.'

'Can I get a train or a bus there to Florence?' said Georgia eagerly.

'Can you drive?'

'Yes. I drive the minibus at the International School.'

He smiled. 'In that case you may have the keys to the car Franco uses for Elsa's marketing.'

Alessa, who expressed a strong wish to accompany Georgia to Florence next day, had to be propitiated by lessons in the summer house, which Georgia allowed now and then as a treat to vary routine. But the day was hotter than usual, with a sultry heaviness to the air, and Georgia cut the lesson short to bring the swimming lesson forward, sure that the weather was building up to a storm.

For the first time since she'd come here, the day dragged so much for Georgia that she greeted Marco Sardi's early arrival home with as much pleasure as Alessa. Thankful that she could go off for a bath with a clear conscience, Georgia left Alessa to her father and Pina and sought the comfort of cool, scented water, wondering if she could plead a headache to avoid a confrontation with Luca at dinner. Then she scowled at herself in the mirror. Coward! Of course she'd go down and behave as though nothing had happened. Nothing much *had* happened, anyway. With any other man a few kisses would have been totally unremarkable. Whereas one touch of Luca's mouth on hers and she'd lost her wits. Her face flamed at the mere thought of it. A good thing Tom had rung at that particular moment, *sconsiderato* or not.

When she arrived downstairs at eight as usual Georgia found that she had nothing to worry about. Luca was not, it seemed, joining them for dinner. Furious at her own disappointment, she did her best to talk normally with Marco, and made no comment on Luca's absence.

Marco, though obliging enough to tell her that Luca was dining with an old friend, omitted to say whether the friend was male or female. Like the day, the meal seemed endless to Georgia, and it was almost a relief when she heard the first rumble of thunder over coffee. Before long the rain was coming down in torrents, and lightning lit up the conservatory with an almost constant display of fireworks.

Although Alessa, she learned, had no fear of thunderstorms Georgia went to bed early, mainly because she was sure that Marco Sardi would consider it bad manners to retire before she did. She detected relief in his weary eyes when she said that she was at the exciting part of the novel she was reading, and took herself off to her room to torture herself with the thoughts of what Luca was doing.

The only fear the spectacular storm inspired was worry over Luca's return through it in the Supremo. He might stay where he was for the night, of course. Georgia couldn't decide which option appealed to her less, and got ready for bed in a state of nerves which the rising crescendo of the storm did little to soothe. She was used to the ferocity of the storms in this part of the world, but this one was particularly melo-dramatic.

She heard Marco Sardi go into his daughter's room next door, as he did every night before he went to bed. In a lull in the thunder she heard his footsteps recede again, then lay on her bed watching the storm through the long windows beside her bed, hoping now that wherever he was, and whoever he was with, Luca would stay there, at least until this father and mother of storms was over.

She thought she heard a car at one point, but couldn't tell if it was Luca in the Supremo. As the storm receded Georgia forced herself to concentrate on the thriller she was reading, and eventually suc-ceeded, mainly because she was about to discover the identity of the killer.

Georgia was so deep in the final denouement that the frantic knocking on the door brought her out of bed with a pounding heart. She threw open the door to find Pina there in her nightgown, her incoherent anguish so great that it took a moment for Georgia to understand the gist of her story. When she did she went white to the lips.

'No, Pina, Alessa is not with me. She must be with her father.'

The girl twisted her hands in utter misery. 'No. Signor Marco went back to Valorino to fetch some papers once the rain stopped. And she is not in his room. I looked.'

'Right.' Georgia pulled herself together and reached for her dressing gown. 'Go and put something on, Pina, then we'll start a proper search. She must be somewhere. Maybe she's gone down to the kitchen for something to eat.'

But Alessa was nowhere in the house. While Pina, hysterical with anguish by this time, went to rouse Elsa and her son Franco, Georgia raced outside to the pool, dreading what she might find there. But the security lights which flashed on at her approach showed her at once that the pool was empty. She went back to join the others, demanding torches.

'It is possible Signor Marco took Alessa with him in the car,' said Franco hopefully.

Georgia, seriously doubting this, suggested that Elsa gave Pina something to calm her down, and put water to heat for hot drinks. Then she told Franco to search the vegetable garden, and all the grounds behind the house, while she covered the lawns and shrubberies and anywhere else she could think of. Suddenly inspiration struck her.

'The summer house!' she said to Franco.

'*Signorina*?'

Georgia gestured down the drive with her torch, searching desperately for the word. '*Il padiglione, il padiglione*!' she cried, and raced off to the remote corner of the grounds where, far beyond the range of the security lights, the summer house lay hidden, high in its copse of cypress.

Georgia hurled herself up the slippery, splintered wooden steps, Franco at her heels as she tried to open the door. 'Alessa!' she screamed, and heard a faint sound in response as she tried to open the door, which had jammed shut.

Franco put her aside, drew back his foot and kicked in the door, and next moment a sobbing, distraught Alessa was clasped fast in Georgia's arms.

'I shouted—but—no one came. I couldn't—open the door,' sobbed the terrified child, while Franco offered up fervent prayers of thankfulness and explained that the rain-swollen door must have slammed shut with a gust of wind, then refused to open again.

'Give her to me, miss,' he said tenderly. 'I will carry her down the steps.'

'Luisa! Luisa!' cried the child, and Georgia shone the torch to look for the doll. She pounced on it, cursing herself for having bought the thing for Alessa in the first place.

'Darling, you came back for her—you should have called me; I would have fetched her for you!' Georgia shone her torch for Franco to make his way safely to the ground with Alessa before trusting her own weight to the stairs, then heard a car roar in through the gates, looked up as she saw headlights, and lost her footing.

She grabbed the handrail, then screamed as the staircase disintegrated beneath her, her flailing hands met empty air and she hurtled to the ground in a welter of creaking, splintering wood. Her breath left her body as she hit the earth, something struck her head with a stunning blow, and Georgia knew no more.

CHAPTER SIX

GEORGIA opened her eyes on a room she'd never seen before. No rioting roses. The walls were covered in ivory watered silk. And she was lying in a tester bed with coral damask curtains caught back with tasselled gilt ropes. Her eyes widened, then shut again quickly against the throbbing pain in her head.

'Ah, you are awake,' said a man's voice in Italian.

Georgia, slow to translate, couldn't find the energy to reply. She nodded. And regretted it. She breathed in sharply, and a cool, dry hand held her wrist to check her pulse.

'Gently, Miss Fleming. Open your eyes, please.' She obeyed, and saw a slim, grey-haired man in a dark suit. He smiled at her encouragingly. 'Keep them open.' He shone a slim torch beam in each eye in turn, then asked if she felt sick.

Georgia thought about it. 'No,' she said doubtfully in English. 'Not really. But my head hurts.'

'A large piece of wood struck it,' he said matter-of-factly.

Georgia, blinded with swift recall of her fall, reared up in sudden alarm.

'Alessa!' she gasped. 'Is she all right? Where is she? Where am *I*?'

'Alessa is perfectly well, Miss Fleming. She is safely asleep in her own bed.' He smiled, easing her gently against the pillows. 'I am Dr Claudio Fassi, and this is merely another room in the Villa Toscana, on the ground floor. Luca brought you here rather than carry you up so many stairs to your own room.'

'Luca?' repeated Georgia faintly.

'Yes. He is waiting impatiently outside the door. Signor Sardi also.' Dr Fassi smiled soothingly. 'You gave everyone a great fright. However, I think you have not come to much harm. You have a lump on your head, and you have sprained an ankle, but you are not, I am certain, concussed. There is no need to convey you to the hospital, as Luca wished.'

Georgia's thinking processes were not at their best. It took her a long time to translate the precise Italian of the doctor, who appeared to understand English but not to speak it.

'You're sure Alessa is all right?' she asked anxiously. 'I remember now. She was shut in the summer house— *il padiglione*,' she added urgently.

Dr Fassi's eyes twinkled. 'She is well, I promise you, and you are improving, Miss Fleming—your Italian is coming back to you.'

She turned her head away in anguish. 'It was all my fault.'

'That the staircase collapsed? I think not! Signor Sardi is very angry with himself for leaving it in disrepair.'

'But it was the doll I brought Alessa which caused it all. She went back to fetch it and got shut in.' Tears trickled from her closed lids. 'Sorry,' she said, sniffing. 'I don't know why I'm crying.'

'You have suffered great anxiety, followed by trauma. A few tears will do you no harm.'

'Everyone says that here,' she said huskily, and opened her eyes. '*Piangi*. Cry. The British say, "Don't cry." '

Dr Fassi smiled kindly. 'You also have a saying, do you not—when in Rome do as the Romans do? Now, my dear, I shall order a tray of weak tea for you, and leave some very mild painkillers for your headache. Two only tonight, please, and no further dose unless absolutely necessary.'

Georgia thanked him hoarsely, watched the door close behind him, then turned her head into the pillow and gave way to tears of weakness, until she heard a husky, familiar voice saying her name urgently.

She turned on her back to look up at Luca and Marco, who were standing by her bed, Luca's eyes burning like blue flames.

Marco Sardi, haggard with anxiety, grasped her hand tightly. 'Georgia, I beg your forgiveness. I knew the steps were unsafe, but I had forgotten them.'

'Please don't apologise. It was an accident.' She scrubbed at her eyes with a tissue from the box on the bedside table. 'You've had more to think about than the summer house lately.'

'You are a kind young lady. But it is no excuse,' he said with remorse. 'I was spared the horror of seeing you fall. It was Luca who arrived on the scene, to find Alessa screaming in the arms of Franco and you unconscious beneath a pile of wood.' He shuddered involuntarily, and Luca put a hand on his arm.

'Marco, enough. I am sure Georgia does not blame you.'

'Luca is right,' she said emphatically. 'I blame myself. I should have noticed when Alessa left the doll behind—'

'Nonsense,' said Luca roughly. 'Besides, who would have imagined that Alessa would have gone out alone into the night to fetch her doll? Pina is afraid of thunder, and the child thought you would be sleeping, Georgia, so she went to get the doll herself. She thinks of herself as the doll's mamma, you see. The person responsible.'

Marco thrust a hand through his silvered dark hair. 'I should be proud that my daughter was both brave and responsible, but all I can think of is that I should have stayed home, and not gone back to Valorino for some figures that could well have waited until Monday—'

'Please, Signor Sardi,' entreated Georgia, then smiled as Elsa appeared with a tray. 'Ah, my tea.'

The atmosphere changed abruptly. Elsa, formidable in a voluminous dark dressing gown, took charge, thrusting pillows behind Georgia and pulling the covers up under her chin with fierce propriety as she suggested that both men would do better to seek their own beds and leave Georgia in peace in hers.

'Here are your pills, my dear,' she said, handing the patient a glass of water. 'I have brought biscuits for you to eat before you drink the tea—on the doctor's instructions,' she added firmly, to quell any signs of insurrection.

Georgia felt too feeble to protest about anything. After both men bade her goodnight, under Elsa's eagle eye she swallowed the pills and nibbled listlessly on a biscuit while the older woman turned off all the lights except the one beside the bed.

'Is Alessa really all right?' Georgia asked anxiously.

'The doctor gave her a little something to make her sleep,' said Elsa soothingly. 'And in the morning, when she sees you are better, she will be very happy, I promise. Perhaps you would like her to eat breakfast with you?'

'Oh, yes, please.' Georgia drank some of her tea, taking in her surroundings as well as she could in the dim light. 'What room is this, Elsa?'

'It is the one kept for Alessa's great-grandmother. She cannot climb stairs, so Signora Sardi made this room specially for the visits of her grandmother.' Elsa stood by the bed, her hands clasped in front of her. 'When Signor Luca brought you in, soaked and unconscious in his arms, I told him to put you here. He was wild enough with fear without having to carry you up several flights of stairs!'

So Luca had been in a bit of a state, which was hardly surprising, considering the drama he'd found when he arrived home. Georgia lifted the covers to find that she was wearing a blush-pink silk nightgown quite unlike anything she owned, and bit her lip in dismay.

'No, no,' said Elsa quickly, misunderstanding. 'It was I who prepared you for bed.'

'Yes, of course. Thank you.' Georgia steeled herself. 'But Elsa, who does the nightgown belong to?'

'Signora Conte, the master's sister. She always leaves things behind when she stays here,' said Elsa, and smiled in reassurance. 'She will not mind.'

Neither did Georgia now. It would have been too painful for words for Alessa to see something once worn by her own mother.

Once she was alone Georgia turned out the light and tried to settle herself to sleep, but in the darkness she kept on reliving the moment when the stairs had given way and she'd hurtled into space. She shivered and reached out and turned on the light, like a child needing a candle in the dark.

Her head, she realised after a while, was better. The ache was receding, the throbbing less violent. She slid wary fingers into her hair to find the lump and grimaced. Either the thickness of her hair had protected her or she had a mortifyingly thick skull. She lay against piled, lace-edged pillows, suddenly depressed as a throb from her ankle warned her that she was unlikely to drive herself to Florence for a while, even less to explore it on foot.

A tap on the door interrupted her musings.

'Come in,' she called quietly, then stared, her eyes wide as Luca came into the room and closed the door softly behind him.

'I saw your light,' he said swiftly as he approached the bed. 'I knew you were awake. I could not sleep until I made sure all was well with you.'

Georgia's heart was beating so hard that she tugged the covers under her chin to hide it. 'I don't feel wonderful,' she said in English. 'I've had some pills, so my head doesn't hurt so much, but it refuses to muster my limited Italian vocabulary.'

He smiled wryly. 'I have no such excuse for my lack of English,' he replied in the same tongue.

It didn't really matter what language they spoke in, Georgia realised. Their eyes were communicating in a way which dispensed with words.

'You frightened me,' he said abruptly. 'For a moment I think—thought you were dead.'

Georgia raised a hand to her head, giving him a rueful little smile. 'It takes more than a block of wood to finish me off, apparently.'

Luca drew nearer, looking down at her in a way which accelerated Georgia's pulse. 'For a moment there in the rain and darkness I could think only that we parted in anger. Then I felt your heart and heard it beating—'

'It's beating now,' she whispered, staring up at him.

Luca bent forward involuntarily, then turned away abruptly. 'Forgive me,' he said in Italian. 'I should not have come here tonight. I told myself I wanted to make sure you had everything you needed, but I lied. To you and to myself.' He turned suddenly to face her, his eyes glowing like sapphires in his set face. 'When I carried you in here you were like a dead thing in my arms. Then Marco came, thank God, to comfort Alessa, but Elsa and Pina took you from me and shut me out. I could not sleep until I had—'

'Had what?' said Georgia gently.

He breathed out, eyes closed, then dropped to his knees beside the bed and slid his arms round her, his cheek against her hair. 'Until I had held you in my arms and felt you warm and alive to my touch,' he said, and raised his head to look down at her. His eyes darkened, and he bent his head to hers, their lips meeting with a mutual gasp of pleasure. Georgia locked her hands behind his head and surrendered herself to the engulfing heat of Luca's kiss, oblivious of throbbing head or any other hurts. She felt a shudder run through Luca's broad chest, and hugged him closer.

'Don't go yet,' she said as he raised his head.

'I don't want to go at all,' he groaned, his mouth against her throat. His lips moved upwards until they found hers, his arms cruelly tight, and Georgia gasped as her head gave a sudden, sickening throb.

Luca jumped up in alarm, looking down into her dilated eyes, which widened to circles of jet in her pale face. 'You feel ill?'

She tried to smile. 'My head just reminded me it hurts, that's all.'

'And I am a brute to behave so when you are still so fragile,' he said with passionate disgust. 'Shall I call Elsa?'

'Certainly not,' said Georgia tartly. 'How would you explain your presence in my room?'

'I had to come,' he said harshly.

'I'm very glad you did.' Her eyes glittered into his. 'I couldn't sleep either. It was a long, miserable day, Luca.'

'For me also.' He clasped her hand in his, his smile turning her bones to liquid.

'Are we friends again?'

'*Friends*?' He gave a smothered laugh. 'Ah, you English! How can you and I be friends, Georgia? You know very well I wish to be your lover.'

The transient glow faded from her face. 'That's out of the question.'

He scowled. 'Why?'

'I'll write out a list of reasons and give them to you tomorrow.'

Their eyes clashed for a moment, then Luca shrugged.

'Forgive me. You are tired and need rest. Tomorrow we will talk again.' His eyes caressed her possessively. 'We shall discuss all these reasons why I should not be your lover, and you will see that none of them will deter me. I want you, Georgia. I want you very, very much.'

'And you always get what you want?'

He nodded, confidence in every line of his tall, graceful body. 'Always!'

Georgia took a long time to get to sleep after the door closed on Luca Valori. The cards, she thought wearily, were well and truly on the table. But for the first time in his life Gianluca Valori would find that there was one thing he couldn't have.

She lay staring at the beautiful room despairingly. If he'd been someone else it would be different. Someone more ordinary. But Luca was the very embodiment of everything she'd ever wanted: looks, charm, intellect, and the ability to set her on fire at his merest touch. This was the stuff all lovers should be made of, thought Georgia bleakly. And he wanted her. But it was what he wanted her *for* that posed the problem.

Georgia lay listing the obstacles that stood in the way of any relationship with Luca Valori. It was out of the question for them to conduct a love affair under Marco Sardi's roof for a start. And once the period of coaching Alessa was over she was going back to her parents until the term began at the school near Venice. The contract for her second year there was already signed, and she had no intention of endangering it, not even for Luca Valori, whose great drawback was the fact that he was so well-known. Mrs Blanchard, the principal of the International School, had made it plain that she required employees with impeccable behaviour on her staff. Which ruled out any dalliance by one of her teachers with a man who had once won the adulation of all Italy for his exploits on the Formula-One circuit.

And there was James, she thought in sudden, horrified remorse. He should have been right at the head of the list. She bit her lip, thinking of the letter she'd received, telling her how much he missed her and how much he was looking forward to seeing her again, once his spell in Cyprus was over. But since she'd met Luca even her weekly letter to James had become a chore.

Burning with guilt and aching all over, unable to put Luca's kisses from her mind, Georgia wrestled with the problem of James, facing the fact that she'd never really been in love with him, and that this, not her career, was her real reason for putting off the wedding. It was a deeply disturbing discovery—one which left her sleepless for the entire, interminable night.

It was a heavy-eyed invalid who welcomed the arrival of Elsa. The brisk, sympathetic woman exclaimed over the rings under Georgia's eyes, helped her hop to the bathroom to save her injured ankle, then brushed the mass of thick fair hair, taking care to avoid the bump.

'You did not sleep well, my dear,' she stated as she settled Georgia back into a swiftly tidied bed.

'No. My head ached.' Georgia smiled gratefully. 'I'm very sorry to cause you more work.'

Elsa snorted. 'Nonsense. I will send Pina and Alessa in with your breakfast tray. But today you drink tea, not coffee,' she warned. 'Dr Fassi instructed me.'

Georgia gazed at the bright day outside, where the sun was shining as though the storm had never happened, then the door opened and Alessa shot across the room, her eyes big with anxiety.

'Georgia, are you better?' she entreated, and Georgia smiled, holding out her arms.

'Yes, I am. But come and give me a hug and I'll be better still!'

The child flung her arms round Georgia's neck and clutched her tightly. 'You fell and hurt your head, and it was all my fault—'

'It was *not* your fault—I just missed my footing. And my head's fine!' said Georgia emphatically. 'Anyway, I should have noticed Luisa was missing and fetched her myself. Ah, look, darling, Pina's bringing our breakfast.'

The girl bade Georgia a shy 'good morning' as she put down a heavily laden tray, enquired after the invalid's health, then put a small table beside the bed and drew a chair up to it for Alessa. The child chattered like a magpie as Pina served the meal.

'If you have everything you want, miss, I shall help Elsa serve breakfast to the master and Signor Luca,' said the maid.

'I can give Georgia anything she needs,' said Alessa importantly, and Georgia chuckled.

'As you see, Pina, I lack for nothing!'

Much reassured by the sight of Georgia apparently little harmed by the adventures of the night, Alessa disposed of a good breakfast, touchingly adult in her efforts to see that the invalid was given every attention.

'I wish I wasn't going to Zia Claudia's today,' she said, once the meal was over. 'I'd rather stay home and look after you.'

'I'll be fine. I'll probably sleep all day.' Georgia smiled affectionately. 'You can impress your cousins with the English words you've learned.'

Alessa looked less than enthusiastic. 'The doctor says you are not to walk for two days,' she informed Georgia. 'You must stay in bed until he comes to see you again.'

'Oh, dear,' sighed Georgia, but secretly she wasn't too unhappy to hear this. She was far from her usual self in more ways than one, and if Marco Sardi was taking his daughter out for the day a long rest in this beautiful bedroom held a very definite appeal. 'Then, if I have to stay here, Alessa, could you fetch some books from my room for me? I shall read so the time will pass quickly while you're away.'

Alessa ran off readily on her errand, and a moment later Marco Sardi arrived with Pina, to enquire after the invalid. He stayed only while Pina was collecting the breakfast things, expressing his regret once more for the faulty stairs, and his relief that Georgia was looking much better than the night before.

She assured him that once her ankle was pronounced fit to walk on she'd be up and about as usual.

'But you should have been driving to Florence today,' he said remorsefully, motioning Pina to remain.

'The museums will still be there when I finally make it,' she said philosophically.

It was mid-morning by the time Dr Fassi arrived. He restrapped Georgia's ankle, examined her thoroughly and pronounced her fit to get up as long as she put no weight on her foot for at least two days. Once Marco Sardi had received assurances from the doctor that the young English lady was a healthy young woman who had taken no lasting harm from her mishap, he brought Alessa in to bid Georgia a reluctant goodbye, then took his daughter off to visit her cousins. By this time it was noon, and Luca was the only one missing from Georgia's list of visitors.

Elsa came bustling in to help Georgia take a bath with one foot out of the water—a process which caused great hilarity and tired Georgia not a little by the time she was dry and cool in a thin pink cotton dress. She sat on the bed with her foot on a stool while Elsa tidied her hair, then looked up in surprise as Luca came in with a knock at the door and flipped her heart over in her chest with his smile.

'She is ready?' he said to Elsa.

'Yes. Lunch will be in half an hour.' The woman smiled, assured a grateful Georgia that it had been a pleasure to help, then went away to the kitchens.

Luca looked even more irresistible than usual to Georgia, in a dazzling white T-shirt and faded old jeans crafted by some master hand, with soft leather moccasins on his bare brown feet. He picked Georgia up in his arms and, ignoring her squeak of surprise, carried her swiftly to the conservatory, where he set her down on a sofa and hooked a stool into place.

'There,' he said, breathing hard. 'Rest your foot.'

Georgia, even more breathless than he, obeyed silently, her colour high as he sat beside her and took hold of her hand.

'How are you this morning?' he asked, in a husky tone caressing enough to ring alarm bells in her brain.

'I'm fine. In fact,' she added, 'I'm not an invalid. Surely there's a walking stick somewhere? You needn't have carried me!'

'You are wrong. I desperately needed to hold you in my arms,' he informed her smugly, so triumphant that she couldn't hold back a smile. 'To hold you close and breathe in the scent of you has taken my breath away. Ah, Georgia. You have such a beautiful smile.'

So do you, she thought silently, gazing at him. 'I was wondering where you were this morning,' she said, then could have bitten her tongue as the triumph deepened on his face.

'You missed me!' he said with satisfaction. 'I knew you would.'

'Is that why you didn't visit the invalid?' She narrowed her eyes at him and he looked pained.

'Of course not. I had to drive to Valorino first, to consult with one of the mechanics this morning. Just so I could devote the rest of the day to you.'

Georgia looked away. The whole day with Luca. Pure bliss—or pure insanity. 'It's very kind of you, but you're not obliged to keep me company,' she said austerely. 'I have books to read, letters to catch up on—which reminds me—may I ring my parents today, please?'

Luca frowned, his blue eyes astonished. 'You have no need to ask. Ring your parents any time you wish. Or anyone else,' he added reluctantly. 'Unless he writes so many letters you need no phone calls to your lover.'

'No point in worrying him. But I'd like to talk to my mother.' She smiled as she waved a hand at her foot. 'I think I'll gloss over last night's experience.'

'Which one?' he asked swiftly. 'Your fall, or the time spent in my arms?'

She glared at him. 'I shan't mention either! Because both of them were isolated occurrences. Neither will happen again.'

Luca leaned back in the corner of the sofa, his long legs stretched out in front of him. He looked at her for a long time in silence, then shook his head slowly.

'It is useless to struggle, Georgia. Fate has brought us together. We are meant to be lovers.'

'No, we are not!' She felt like a sitting duck, marooned on the sofa with no chance of getting away. 'Even if I—I wanted to I wouldn't dream of repaying Signor Sardi's kindness by behaving so badly under his roof. He hired me to teach his daughter, remember. Which is all academic anyway. You've forgotten about James.'

'I have not,' he said grimly. 'Nor Tom Hannay.'

Georgia glowered at him. 'Will you *please* forget Tom?'

'Promise to do the same and I will.'

At which point Pina arrived to lay the table for lunch, and all hostilities were temporarily suspended. By the time Elsa arrived, with *crostini* for their first course, and bade Luca carry Georgia to the table, both of them had cooled down somewhat, and Georgia was able to enjoy the paté-spread toast more than she'd expected to in the circumstances.

They were obliged to talk of impersonal subjects while Pina cleared plates and brought wine and mineral water, then returned with plates of *arrosta*, rosemary-flavoured roast pork, served with artichokes drizzled with the matchless local olive oil.

The meal had been cleared away, Georgia had drunk the tea the doctor advised, Luca had downed several cups of black coffee, and she had been lulled into believing that he meant to drop the subject, when he resumed their conversation as though there had been no break in it at all.

'We *shall* become lovers,' he said conversationally, startling her. 'I believe fate has brought us together for just this purpose, Georgia.'

'This isn't fair,' she said with sudden passion. 'For the moment I can't even walk, let alone run away from you.'

He gazed at her in surprise. 'Why should you run away from me?'

She sighed in exasperation. 'Can't I make you understand? Just because you want something doesn't mean you can have it. I don't *want* to be your lover, Luca Valori.'

'You lie,' he said, unmoved, and picked her up, holding her high against his chest. 'See? It is you who are breathless.' He bent his head and kissed her mouth before she could turn away. 'What would you like to do now? Shall I take you back to your room for a rest?'

'Yes, please,' she said in a stifled voice. She kept her head turned away from him as he carried her back through the hall and along the corridor that led to his grandmother's room. He laid her on the bed, propped pillows behind her and bent until his lips rested on hers, light but sure, and very possessive. He raised his head to gaze down into her dark, wary eyes. 'I will come back for you later, when the sun is less fierce. We shall have tea together in the garden. I shall call Elsa now, and she will help you to bed.'

Georgia, helpless against the rock-solid wall of his assurance, hated the sensation, yet when he bent his head to kiss her again she couldn't resist him, and he knew it. She had to clench her hands to stop them locking round his neck. Luca raised his head at last, breathing raggedly, his eyes molten as they clashed with hers. He stood up slowly, his mouth curving in a smile of such intimacy that she flushed scarlet. 'Sleep,' he said, in the deep, caressing voice which was a seduction in itself, then he went swiftly from the room.

Sleep! Georgia sat upright and gingerly put one foot on the floor, then looked up in alarm as the door opened again. But it was Elsa who came in.

'Don't put weight on that foot,' scolded the house-keeper. 'Come. I shall help you to the bathroom, then you must rest.'

Later, cool in the exquisite satin nightgown, and tucked neatly beneath a fresh linen sheet, Georgia lay against the pillows feeling as though a lot more than a flight of steps had fallen on top of her.

Luca Valori wanted her, and was accustomed to victory in more ways than on the racing track, it was obvious. It was going to be very difficult to hold out against him. Mainly because every instinct yearned to give in. And he knew it. But it just wasn't possible. Luca was a dream lover. Unfortunately a dream lover of enough substance to make her almost forget James. She tried to conjure up James's fair, angular face, but it was blurred and indistinct, like an old photograph, quickly superimposed by the imperious features of Gianluca Valori.

Luca Valori's intentions, of course, had nothing to do with marriage or any other kind of commitment. And, to do him justice, he'd never tried to mislead her that they were. A love affair with Alessa's English teacher would be nothing more than a little diversion for him before he settled down to perpetuate the Valori dynasty with some suitable Tuscan beauty.

CHAPTER SEVEN

THE thought was surprisingly hard to bear, to the point of causing unwanted tears to slide down Georgia's cheeks. She scrubbed them away fiercely, assuring herself that they were perfectly natural—just the aftermath of the episode the night before. She thrust all thought of Luca away, and did her best to relax, but, although Elsa had closed the blinds firmly, to encourage sleep, it was some time before Georgia drifted at last into an uneasy doze.

She woke from it with a start to find someone bending over her, and uttered a cry which was stifled by a warm, seeking mouth that ignited a stab of involuntary response before she woke fully, panicking, and tried to push Luca away. He overcame her resistance with ease, as though he'd expected it and was having no nonsense with any opposition. She shivered as it dawned on her that he'd made his declaration of intent at lunch and now he was here to follow it up.

'Do not worry, *carissima*,' he said, the mixture of English and Italian strangely seductive in the deep, caressing voice. 'You are half-asleep still, so we shall use your language—until the time for talking is over.'

At this Georgia, very much awake, renewed her struggles in earnest, but he laughed, restraining her effortlessly.

'Stop it!' she panted. 'I meant what I said. I won't— you can't—'

'I can and I will,' he assured her, and returned his mouth to hers, stifling her protests with lips which caressed and cajoled as he drew her up into a powerful embrace, one arm holding her close while his free hand smoothed and soothed, running down her spine with a practised, delicate touch that she felt like a trickle of fire through the thin, borrowed silk. For a few throbbing, breathless moments Georgia yielded mindlessly to him, then from somewhere summoned up the fast-evaporating will to push him away.

'Elsa!' she choked.

Luca pushed her against the pillows, and lay down, his arms locked around her. 'Franco has driven Pina and Elsa into Lucca for the shopping,' he said in a voice hoarse with desire. 'We shall not be disturbed, *tesoro*.'

To her dismay Georgia found herself trembling violently, assailed by a mixture of so many emotions that it was hard to separate one from the other. 'I—can't—believe this!' she panted.

'That I desire you?' he whispered, and bent his head to touch his tongue to the places his hands laid bare. Hot darts of response shot through her, performing the double feat of turning her both liquid with desire and tense with fury at her own uncontrollable response.

'No—*aah*.' Her breath left her in a groan of anguish as his clever hands wrought such exquisite havoc that she could scarcely endure it. 'Luca, please—'

'Ah, *carissima*, you are so beautiful, so perfect in my arms—I want you so desperately; do not fight me!' His voice was so deep and husky with desire that it struck an answering chord deep inside her. She tried to ignore it, to protest, but Luca silenced her with his mouth and hands, caressing her to a fever pitch of response until she was overwhelmed by so great a tide of longing that when at last Luca took possession of her, with such ease and mastery, she gasped for an instant at the sudden, thrilling shock of it before the reality of what was happening revitalised her into frantic, futile opposition.

But it was too late. His superbly fit body was programmed for conquest and release, and all too soon Luca gasped in the climactic throes of the passion which rendered him blind and deaf to her entreaties.

Then it was over. Georgia pushed him away with hands that shook. Luca Valori sat up, still breathing hard, his colour high and his eyes glittering as they met the bitter resentment in hers. He slid from the bed, pulling on the clothes she'd never even noticed him take off. She averted her head, pulling the sheet up under her chin.

'*Carissima*—' he said urgently.

'Just go,' she said, in a voice so quietly bitter that he leaned over her and took her hand. She snatched it away, and dark colour rose in his face.

'We must talk,' he pressed. 'You are angry that this has happened, but I was so sure—'

'Sure of what?' she snapped.

'That you felt the same desire for me as I do for you,' he said simply, buttoning his shirt. 'Your words said no, but your body said yes. Admit it, Georgia. Because,' he added softly, his eyes meeting hers, 'it would not have been physically possible to take possession of you with such rapture if you had felt no desire for me.'

Georgia bit her lip in mortification. He was right, of course. She *had* wanted him. 'I just didn't think you'd really take advantage of the fact,' she said hoarsely. 'I wanted you to kiss me, and touch me, but not—not—' She swallowed convulsively, her free hand to her head as the colour drained suddenly from her face.

Luca leapt to her side. *'Che cosa—?'*

'My head.' She thrust a hand into her tangled hair. 'Go away, please. *Now*!'

Georgia felt his hand on her hair and flinched away, heard him mutter a muffled oath. At last the door closed behind him, and she threw the sheet back and got out of bed, clutching at the bedpost for support. Hopping and limping in turn, she made it to the bathroom, turned on the hot water, then lay in it as hot as she could bear it, wishing that she could stay where she was for the foreseeable future.

When she struggled out at last, wrapped in a bath-towel, she hobbled to the doorway, then paused, bristling with hostility as she found Luca waiting for her, showered and immaculate in pale linen trousers and one of his inevitable blue shirts. Without a word he picked her up and carried her to the chaise longue at the foot of the bed.

'You took the bandage off,' he said, eyeing the bruised, swollen ankle.

'I had a very necessary bath,' she returned bitterly.

'I will send Elsa—'

'No!'

'Yes. She has returned.' His eyes met hers. 'When I left you Elsa was escorting my grandmother into the house. Nonna saw me leave this room and asked why I was there. It is her room when she stays here, you understand. Elsa explained about you. My grandmother demanded my reasons for being alone with you in your room, and drew her own conclusions. She was—not pleased.'

Georgia closed her eyes in despair. 'You didn't tell her what happened?'

'No. You think I am a fool?' Luca's mouth twisted. 'But of course—you do. I told her very little. But I fear she assumes much.'

She groaned in horror. 'Then I must leave at once.'

'You cannot!' he said fiercely. 'In your condition—'

'You ignored my *condition* earlier on!' Georgia flung at him. Luca flinched, then turned on his heel and strode from the room. A moment later Elsa came in with an armful of clothes, put them down on a chest, took one look at Georgia and folded her in a firm embrace.

'Cry,' she commanded.

Georgia, much heartened by this treatment, obeyed for a moment or two then found she didn't want to cry any more. Elsa smoothed the tumbled fair hair back from Georgia's face. 'Come. I am to help you dress, then you are to take tea in the conservatory with Signora Valori.'

'Oh, *no!*' Georgia shuddered, but knew that there was no way of avoiding the interview with Luca's grandmother.

She let Elsa bind her ankle again, then put on fresh underwear and the demure pink dress. She sat still meekly while her hair was brushed, then requested her handbag from the bedside table and made a few repairs to her face—to Elsa's disapproval.

'After such an experience why tire yourself with such things?'

'I need it to boost my morale,' said Georgia.

'Signora Valori is a very kind lady. You need not fear her.'

Georgia gave a wry smile. 'I'm not frightened. Just embarrassed. I wish I could run away and hide.'

Elsa made soothing noises, then went from the room to fetch Luca. He came quickly, grimly silent after a look at Georgia's cold, withdrawn face. He bent down and scooped her up in his arms and carried her, still in silence, to the conservatory where Emilia Valori sat enthroned behind a silver tray.

The elegant old lady stared in surprise as Luca carried his burden in and set her down on a chair by the table, then pulled out a stool for Georgia's foot. 'Nonna, this is the young lady engaged to give Alessa English lessons.'

'How do you do, *signora*?' said Georgia, flushing. 'I sprained my ankle.'

At the look on his grandmother's face Luca's handsome mouth compressed. 'She did so last night, in the accident I described to you, Nonna,' he said harshly. 'Not as a result of my attentions.'

'I am deeply relieved to hear it. Now present us properly, please.'

Georgia felt as though she was living through some surreal dream as Luca Valori presented her to his grandmother with formality, for all the world as though this were a tea-party where the two women had only just met.

'You speak our language well, Miss Fleming,' said Signora Valori, and gestured at the tray. 'Will you take tea or coffee?'

'She is forbidden coffee,' put in Luca.

'I'd love some coffee,' Georgia said flatly, ignoring him, and the other woman smiled and filled a cup with strong black liquid, then, without consulting Georgia, added a spoonful of sugar.

'It will do you good,' she said firmly, and fixed her tall, grim grandson with a look. 'I think it best if you leave us, Luca.'

'Nonna—' he began urgently, but the small, elegantly dressed head shook in refusal.

'You are in no position to object.'

Luca paused in front of Georgia. 'This is not my idea, you understand.'

She looked up at him in frozen silence, and with the usual lift of his shoulder he gave a brief, unsmiling bow to each lady and strode out into the garden.

'And now he will drive that dangerous machine along the *autostrada* and try to channel all his anger and shame into speed.' Signora Valori shook her head, and fixed Georgia with a commanding blue eye. 'Now then, Miss Fleming, I met my grandson emerging from the room you are occupying since your accident. No one was in the house at the time, so, tell me, did you invite him there?'

'No, I did not,' said Georgia expressionlessly.

Signora Valori eyed Georgia thoughtfully. 'Tell me, did you give Gianluca cause to believe his advances might be welcome?'

It took a moment or two for her meaning to sink in. Georgia's chin lifted. 'If you mean was I attracted to your grandson, then the answer is yes.' She sighed deeply. 'After my fall my common sense deserted me, I admit. We were both shocked and—and upset by the accident, and we exchanged a few kisses. If that is what you mean by encouragement, then I suppose I am partly to blame. He was quite frank about wanting—wanting to be my lover.' She bit her lip miserably. 'I made the mistake of saying that it was impossible, never dreaming that he'd take it as a challenge. That it would lead to what happened just now.'

'Then he did make love to you,' said Signora Valori quietly.

Georgia stared at her in dismay. 'Didn't he tell you that?'

'No. He refused to give his reasons for being in your room. You have merely confirmed my suspicions.' The old lady sighed. 'So, Miss Fleming, may I ask what you want from Gianluca by way of reparation?'

'Nothing whatsoever—thank you,' added Georgia belatedly. 'Unless you could persuade him to move out of the Villa Toscana until I leave for England.'

'I am sure that could be arranged.' Signora Valori frowned. 'But when you have time to think, my dear, you may find you need more than that.'

Georgia put down her coffee-cup with a hand which shook.

'Forgive me,' went on her inquisitor relentlessly, 'but may I ask how old you are, Miss Fleming? Were you a virgin before meeting with Luca?'

'I'm twenty-six,' said Georgia, and smiled bitterly. 'And this was not, as you so rightly suspect, my first experience of—of sex. I am virtually engaged to James Astin, who is a captain in the British Army. I've been in no hurry to marry him, because I wanted a career of my own before settling down to be an army wife.'

'And in the meantime you met my grandson.' The old lady sighed. 'Did Luca know you were not indifferent to him?'

'Yes.' Georgia flushed. 'He knew. But I told him that any relationship of the kind he wanted was out of the question.'

'Why?' asked Signora Valori.

Georgia stared at her blankly. 'I would have thought that was obvious. I won't lie to you. I was deeply tempted. But I couldn't throw away the prospect of a perfectly suitable marriage just because Gianluca Valori wanted me for a—a playmate for a while. Also I have a job at a school near Venice. The principal is a strict lady. She would probably dispense with my services if she knew I was mad enough to have an affair with any man during my employment—let alone a man idolised nationwide for his exploits on the Grand Prix circuit.'

'I see,' said the other woman thoughtfully, her slim black brows drawn together below her coiled white hair. 'And are you wondering if such a fiasco could have consequences?'

Georgia nodded miserably, and Signora Valori raised a shoulder in a familiar mannerism.

'Who knows? Nature can be very cruel, bestowing children on those who do not wish for them and depriving others who want them desperately. But I trust,' she added with emphasis, 'that if a child should result from Luca's attentions you will inform him.'

Panic rose in Georgia at the mere thought of it. She didn't want a child. Not now, not like this. 'There's probably no cause for concern,' she said firmly, then smiled at Signora Valori. 'I'm sure you'll be interested to learn how well Alessa's doing with her English.'

'By which I am to take it the subject is closed,' said the old lady wryly. 'Very well, Miss Georgia Fleming, we shall say no more. For the moment.' She opened

a small handbag and took out a card to hand to
Georgia. 'Here is my telephone number and address.
Contact me at any time. Should you need to.'

She sighed heavily. 'Incidentally, my dear, believe
it best for all concerned if Marco knows nothing of
this afternoon's incident. He cannot remedy it, and
he is very attached to Luca. It would merely add to
his burden of grief over my Maddalena.' For a
moment the autocratic little face looked old and
weary. 'Do you agree?'

'Wholeheartedly,' Georgia assured her.

Emilia Valori nodded in approval, sat even more
erect, and gave Georgia a determined smile. 'Now I
shall do as you so obviously want, and discuss my
great-granddaughter. Is she as clever as Marco
believes?'

There was much activity in the villa that evening as
Elsa prepared a special dinner in honour of Signora
Valori, served earlier than usual so that Alessa could
stay up for it.

'I had not meant to remain here longer than an hour
or so,' the old lady told Georgia, 'because I am *en
route* to Siena to stay with my sister. However, I think
it best I stay to see Alessa. Also I would like another
word with Luca. I have rung Vittoria to explain and
will arrive in Siena after dinner instead of before.'

'I'm glad,' said Georgia gratefully. 'Will *you* ask
Luca not to tell Signor Sardi about—about this
afternoon?'

'At first I thought to give him orders on the subject.'
The blue eyes twinkled. 'But I will make it a request.
Luca does not take orders kindly. Will you ring the

bell for Pina, my dear? I have something you may find very useful for a day or two.'

Pina was sent to ask Signora Valori's chauffeur for the spare ebony walking stick always kept in the car.

'Thank you,' said Georgia with fervour. 'Now I shan't feel so helpless.'

When she returned to the ground-floor room Georgia found that the bed had been stripped and remade, even to a fresh counterpane. Her clothes had been brought downstairs and hung in the wardrobe, and after the rest recommended by Signora Valori she changed into the black dress worn for her first night.

The effect was somewhat marred by wearing only one black linen pump, but Georgia shrugged philosophically, made up her face with great care, then gingerly brushed her hair into a smooth, shining coil which she secured with an onyx and gilt clasp. As she laid down the brush she heard cars drive up and then Alessa shouting 'Bisnonna!' at the top of her voice as she rushed to the conservatory to greet her great-grandmother.

Georgia threaded her pearl drops through her ears, then stiffened as she heard a tap on the door. But it was Pina who put a head round it, smiling shyly.

'Signor Luca is asking when you wish to be carried to dinner, Signorina.'

So Luca was back.

Georgia flourished the ebony stick, smiling brightly. 'Tell him I can manage on my own now, thank you, Pina.'

Determined to suffer the tortures of the damned rather than accept help from Luca, Georgia limped slowly across the hall, leaning heavily on the stick, her teeth sunk in her bottom lip with effort as she negotiated the gleaming wood floor.

'*Stupidità!*' said a voice roughly, and without ceremony Luca tossed the stick on a long crimson sofa and scooped her up in his arms. 'You are prepared to risk further damage to your ankle rather than let me help you?' he demanded, glaring into her stormy eyes.

'Yes,' she snapped.

'We need to talk,' he stated grimly as he strode with her along the passageway to the conservatory.

'No, we don't. There's nothing to be said.' She turned her head away, then all further private conversation was suspended as Alessa came running to meet them, her face blazing with excitement because she was allowed to stay up to dinner.

'Are you better, Georgia?' she asked anxiously as Luca set his unwilling burden down on a chair near Signora Valori.

'Darling, I'm fine. It's just this silly foot. I'll be running around as fast as you in a day or two.' Georgia kissed the flushed little cheek, then gave a belated greeting to Signora Valori and Marco Sardi.

'Did you enjoy the peace and quiet this afternoon?' asked Marco kindly.

'Yes, indeed,' said Georgia in a strangled tone, and bent to examine her foot in embarrassment.

'Give her some champagne, Luca,' said his grandmother quickly. 'It is my weakness,' she added as Georgia straightened. 'I allow myself one glass a week. Tonight I may even have two.'

'Is this a celebration of some kind, Emilia?' asked Marco, amused.

'It's not often you have an English guest,' she returned blandly, and smiled at Georgia. 'We spent a very interesting afternoon together.'

'So your peace and quiet was short-lived,' he said to Georgia, who was beginning to wish she'd stayed in her room.

Fortunately the presence of Alessa prevented any lasting awkwardness, since she sat on Luca's knee and gave him a blow-by-blow account of her visit to her cousins, boasting of their amazement at her prowess in their swimming pool.

'You have done well, Georgia,' said Signora Valori in an undertone. 'Alessa is a different child.'

Luca glanced up sharply at the hint of familiarity between the two women, and Georgia turned her head away quickly, stiff with resentment at the mere sight of those brilliant blue eyes.

'Are you sure you feel well?' asked Marco, frowning. 'You look very flushed, Georgia.'

She smiled brightly. 'It's the champagne.'

Georgia was seated between Marco Sardi and Alessa at dinner, with Luca opposite, beside his grandmother. Each time she looked up she found his eyes trained on her, and to avoid them she engrossed herself in Alessa's account of her day, which had included impressing her cousins with the tale of her adventure in the storm.

'I told them I cried and cried when the stairs fell on you,' said Alessa, too excited to eat more than a few mouthfuls of the food put in front of her.

'It is lucky Georgia has only a sprained ankle,' said Luca abrasively. 'I had no idea those stairs were so unsafe.'

'It was always my intention to have them repaired,' said Marco remorsefully. 'But lately—' He broke off, shrugging, and Signora Valori smiled at him kindly.

'Luckily there was no harm done, Marco.'

Georgia glared at Luca for adding to the lines on Marco Sardi's face. 'It was my fault for forgetting the doll,' she said with emphasis.

Luca said very little from that point on—something which, by his puzzled look, Marco Sardi was very much aware of as he noted the tension on his brother-in-law's handsome face. It was left to Signora Valori to keep the conversation flowing, and only Alessa commented on her uncle's silence.

'Are you all right, Luca?' she asked anxiously, and he smiled with genuine warmth at his niece, his eyes tender.

'I am very well, thank you, my darling,' he assured her. 'And, because Georgia has hurt her foot, to-morrow *I* shall take you swimming in the pool.'

Alessa was so pleased with this promise that she made no objection when Pina came to collect her to put her to bed. She bestowed kisses on everyone, asked her great-grandmother to come again soon, then went off with the maid, leaving the others to their coffee.

'In a few minutes I must leave,' said Signora Valori, looking suddenly weary. 'It is quite wonderful to see Alessa so animated and cheerful again, Marco.'

He nodded gravely. 'I am grateful to Georgia. She has been very good for my little one.'

'Alessa will miss her,' agreed the old lady, getting to her feet.

'We shall all miss her,' said Luca as he leapt to assist her.

'Then perhaps she will stay a little longer, if everyone is very kind to her,' said Emilia Valori with significance. She bent over Georgia and kissed her on both cheeks. 'Goodbye, my dear. Remember what I said.'

Georgia was left alone at the table, feeling suddenly weary and homesick and in great need of her mother. Her ankle throbbed in unison with the bump on her head, and she looked up in appeal as Elsa came to clear away.

'What is it?' said the woman quickly. 'Do you need the bathroom?'

'I need to go to bed,' said Georgia thickly. 'Could you fetch my stick, please, Elsa?'

'Of course, of course. I shall help you—and tell Signor Sardi you were tired.'

In minutes Georgia was lying in the wide, cool bed, propped up on pillows with her hair brushed loose, a tray with tea and cold drinks beside her and a book in her lap. Released from the effort to smile and make conversation, slowly she began to relax, to put the events of the day into perspective. It was, she decided, impossible to erase the episode with Luca from her mind. She would go over it dispassionately instead, rather than let it assume nightmare proportions in some locked mental compartment.

For the first time Georgia let herself dwell on what had happened, to view the episode with Luca objectively. Because, although Luca had taken her by surprise, at a time when she was half-asleep and in a vulnerable state after the accident, it was useless to deny her ultimate response to him—a response she'd never felt before, certainly not on the relatively few occasions that she'd shared a bed with James, she realised, depressed.

What made one man's lovemaking so different from another's? Chemistry, presumably. But the biggest surprise had been her utter helplessness against the driving force of a man determined to be her lover. It showed very graphically how lucky she'd been never to have run up against it before.

Admittedly the sprained ankle had been a contributing factor in her lack of defence. But there was more to it than that. In Luca's arms she'd experienced rapture as well as resentment at male domination and his utter confidence in her willingness. And, she thought wearily, she'd learned something else too. Even if she never laid eyes on Gianluca Valori in her life again, marriage with James was no longer possible.

The realisation banished sleep altogether. Despite her headache and deep reluctance for the task, she forced herself to write to James immediately to tell him so. The letter took a long time, with a lot of discarded notepaper before she finally made it clear to James, as tactfully and gently as possible, that she could never be his wife.

Utterly exhausted afterwards, feeling like a murderer, Georgia picked up her book and tried to read, half her attention on the sounds of a household retiring to bed. Elsa and Pina, she knew, retired early on Saturday nights to go to church early on Sunday mornings. Luca's whereabouts she refused to dwell on.

After another hobbling, painful trip to the bathroom Georgia returned to bed, to read again in an attempt to woo sleep, but it was impossible. Guilt over James, not least because she kept thinking of Luca instead, kept her wide awake. Would Luca leave the villa as she'd asked? He must have another home somewhere, because it was obvious that he'd only moved into the Villa Toscana after his sister died. If it weren't for Alessa, of course, the simplest solution would be to leave the villa herself. She thought about it at length, but couldn't bear the thought of hurting Alessa by leaving earlier than arranged. As it was, the parting would be hard enough when the time came.

It was an hour after midnight when Georgia stretched out her hand to turn off the lamp, then froze as she saw the door open. She held her breath, her heart hammering as Luca came into the room and shut the door noiselessly behind him.

CHAPTER EIGHT

'I WILL not harm you further, I swear,' said Luca harshly. 'But I must talk to you.'

Georgia gave him a hostile stare. 'Then please speak English. I'm too tired to struggle with a foreign language tonight. Besides, there's nothing to say.'

His jaw tightened. 'There is much to say,' he replied, switching to English, his accent marked as he searched for the right words. 'I begin by expressing my regret for what happened. It was a mistake.'

'A *mistake*?' she said, incensed.

He shrugged impatiently. 'If you insist on English I may not use the right words. Yes, it was a mistake. But you must understand—you possess for me something I have not met before in a woman. It drove me to madness today. Perhaps the accident last night sent me crazy. Suddenly it was agony to think of you with this James of yours—Tom Hannay also. I wanted—*needed*—to show you what love could be like between you and me, that I could make you forget both of them in my arms. And when you yielded to my kisses so—so ravishingly I thought—I believed—'

'I would welcome you into my bed with open arms once everyone was out of the way today,' she said brutally, and had the satisfaction of seeing dark colour rush into his face.

Luca turned away, but only to fetch a chair. 'You permit?' he said formally, and at her shrug of indifference seated himself as if prepared for a long discussion. 'I know that in your country customs are different,' he began slowly. 'Your religion, certain attitudes—'

'Towards sex, you mean,' she said without emotion. 'You thought that because I'm twenty-six years old, with a reasonable face and figure, and independent enough to take a job in a foreign country, I was sure to have a string of lovers as well as James. One more, you thought, would make very little difference.'

'That is not true,' he said hotly, and leaned forward, his eyes blazing into hers. 'I believed only one lover, though I also suspected your *cognato*, this Tom Hannay. I desired to make you forget all men but me. It was not my intention to—' He stopped, and breathed in deeply. 'Please believe me, Georgia! I wanted you badly. *Dio*, I still do. You had kissed me, here in this room after the accident; I held you in my arms and you responded to me; my need for you was like fire in my blood. I thought—'

'In Grand Prix terms you thought you were in pole position,' she said scathingly, and turned her head on the pillow wearily. 'It's all right, Gianluca Valori. I absolve you of guilt. After the accident I suppose I wasn't quite sane myself. You took me by surprise when you kissed me here last night.' Georgia turned back to him with a sardonic little smile. 'But it never occurred to me that you'd actually follow the kisses up right here under your brother-in-law's roof. Heavens above, Luca, I've got a sprained ankle, a bump on my head *and* I'm in your grandmother's bed.'

'I know, I know,' he threw back at her, scowling blackly. He raked a hand through his thick dark hair. 'But last night I thought at first you were dead. Then

I found you were not.' He drew in a deep, unsteady breath, his eyes brilliant as they locked with hers. 'From the moment I first saw you on the plane I desired you, then today, to have you helpless in my arms—' He shrugged morosely. 'I lost my head.'

'Don't worry, I shan't sue,' she said bleakly.

'Sue? What is that?'

Georgia thought for a moment. *'Citare in giudizio?'*

'You have no need for the law!' he retorted, and sprang to his feet, his face dark with offence. 'I am a Valori. We pay our debts. Tell me what you want of me and it is yours.'

She looked at him in silence, then smiled faintly. 'Anything?'

Luca Valori stood like a man facing a firing-squad. 'Anything.'

'Then I think I have the right to demand—' Georgia paused tantalisingly, enjoying the tension in his face '—your absence.'

He looked thunderstruck. *'Cosa?'*

'Your absence,' she repeated patiently. 'I want you to leave the Villa Toscana and stay away until I go home in three weeks' time. You can visit Alessa on my days off,' she added. 'Elsa can ring you to let you know when I go out.'

'But Alessa wants me here. You will not be so cruel to the child,' he added, with such triumph that Georgia could have hit him.

'With me here she won't mind so much. And you did say "anything",' she reminded him. 'Are you going back on your word?'

'No, I am not!' Gianluca Valori gave her a fulminating look and strode to the door. He opened it, then turned to look at her. 'My grandmother told me you wanted me to go, but I did not believe her. She told me I was fortunate. That some women would be demanding money, or, worse, even marriage, in the circumstances.'

'I've already got a bridegroom, just waiting for me to name the day,' Georgia said, fingers crossed under the sheet. That once James received her letter this would no longer be true was nothing at all to do with Luca.

'So?' He smiled sceptically. 'If *I* proposed marriage I think you might send this soldier of yours away.'

Georgia went white with rage. 'You can think what you like! Nevertheless, I don't want you for a husband, nor do I want any money from you. I can earn my own. So goodbye.'

'Goodbye?' He stared at her incredulously. 'You mean this?'

'Yes.'

He came back to the bed, looking down at her flushed face, at the mass of fair, tumbled hair, and suddenly his eyes flamed. Before she realised his intention he reached down and pulled her up into his arms, his mouth bruising hers with a punitive, angry kiss. Georgia lay limp against him. Instinct told her that resistance was unwise. If she fought, Luca might decide to carry on where he'd left off, and one way and another that would be a very bad idea.

'No,' he said harshly, reading her mind. 'I will not add to my crime. But if this is goodbye I will make sure you remember me.'

He bent his head and kissed her again, but this time with such passionate enticement that she failed to control a shiver of response, and he caught her close

against him in the crook of one arm while his free
hand slid over the satin covering her breasts. She
gasped and he made a smothered sound deep in his
throat, his kiss deepening until her senses reeled and
she would have given her soul to throw her arms round
his neck and repeat the experience of the afternoon.
But pride and sanity kept her rigid in his embrace,
and after a moment Luca laid her against the pillows,
his breathing hurried as he straightened to stare down
at her.

'Very well, English teacher. I will go tomorrow. It
goes hard with me to submit so tamely. But I gave
my word.' He waited for a moment, then, when she
said nothing, he lifted a shoulder in his usual, negligent shrug and strode from the room.

Next morning Pina arrived alone with the breakfast
tray, to report that Alessa would be in later. She was
breakfasting with her father and uncle, because Signor
Luca was going away for a while.

'Really?' said Georgia lightly. 'A business trip?'

'No, miss. He is going to his house. Some building
repairs are needed there.'

'Oh.' Georgia fought with her curiosity and lost.
'Where does he live?'

'In the hills a few kilometres from here.' Pina
poured tea, then began tidying the room. 'The house
was a farm once. Signor Luca has done a lot of work
on it.'

Georgia asked no more questions, much as she'd
have liked to, and when Alessa came running to see
her she had managed to shower and dress and was
ready to hobble to the conservatory with the aid of
her stick. Marco Sardi was waiting for her to enquire

how she was, and Georgia assured him that she was almost fully recovered.

'Even so, do not overdo things today,' he advised. 'Dr Fassi will call this afternoon. By the way,' he added, 'Luca sends his good wishes for your recovery, but he will be away for a time. His house needs attention, he says.'

'So Pina told me.' Georgia sat down on a sofa, smiling gratefully as Alessa rushed to place a stool under the injured foot. 'Thank you, darling.'

'I will look after Georgia, Papa,' she assured her father. 'And I will be very good.'

Marco Sardi laughed indulgently, and kissed his child lovingly. 'Then I may go to Valorino with a light heart!'

Having demanded Luca's absence, Georgia found that she missed him quite desperately. Without his company to look forward to in the evenings life was suddenly flat. Her main consolation was the rapid improvement in her ankle. By the end of the week she was walking without a stick, but the doctor advised against a return to her old room, saying improvement would be swifter without several trips a day up two flights of stairs.

Georgia was sorry. To remain in the bed where Luca had held her naked in his arms was no help in putting the incident from her mind. And to her deep dismay she went on missing him more and more as each day passed. Marco Sardi came home each night, scrupulously passing on good wishes for her health from Luca, and Georgia accepted them politely, hoping that he couldn't tell that the very mention of Luca's name made her pulse race and her appetite decrease.

Since Marco Sardi seemed to eat less and less each day, and Georgia was little better, Elsa became quite voluble on the subject and demanded to know if there was something wrong with her cooking. Assured that her food was superlative, as always, she confided to Georgia next day that the master was worrying her.

'He is still grieving,' she said darkly. 'Without the *signora* he is like a lost soul. Only Alessa keeps him alive, I think.'

Even allowing for a touch of Latin drama, Georgia could see that Elsa had good cause for worry, and assured her employer that she was quite happy to remain at the villa over the weekend if he needed rest instead of spending the time with Alessa.

'No, my dear. Certainly not. You must go on your postponed trip to Florence. I enjoy time spent with my daughter; also Luca is joining us for lunch. You can leave us alone with a clear conscience.' His eyes twinkled. 'When you go for good we shall have to manage without you, remember.'

'Yes, of course,' she said automatically, her enthusiasm for Florence diminished by the prospect of missing Luca.

'Georgia,' he went on, stirring sugar into his coffee. 'You would tell me if there was something wrong, I hope.'

She looked at him, startled. 'Wrong?'

He shrugged. 'You eat less than I these days, and Luca is irritable and withdrawn and working like a man possessed at the *fabbrica*. I have no wish to intrude on your private concerns, but while you are under my roof I naturally feel responsible for your welfare. I know Luca is attracted to you. Then suddenly he says he must go. That his house needs his attention. I do not believe it. I think you had a quarrel. And if you have been offended in any way I wish to know.'

'There's nothing wrong, I assure you,' said Georgia, feeling utterly wretched at the lie. 'And my lack of appetite stems from lack of exercise. I'm now good as new and shortly I'll be eating like a horse again.'

Marco Sardi looked unconvinced. 'Very well, my dear. If you say so. Now let us talk of arrangements for tomorrow. Unfortunately Franco needs the car. But he will take you to the station and you can go by train to Florence. Then either he or I will pick you up again when you return.'

'I'd prefer that,' said Georgia truthfully. 'Dr Fassi advised against driving for another week, so the train will be fine. I've got maps and a guidebook, so Florence, here I come!'

Georgia was up at the crack of dawn next day, bade an affectionate farewell to a sleepy Alessa, then went off with Franco to catch the train to Florence in the gold heat haze of a Tuscan summer morning.

She enjoyed the journey and got off the train at Stazione Santa Maria Novella in Florence. Guidebook in hand, she hurried off among the other passengers, but slowed down as she reached the tempting windows of expensive shops set in the Renaissance buildings and *palazzi* of the Via Tornabuoni. Then, after consultation with her map, she made her way to the great Piazza della Signoria, and the Uffizi, the treasure house of Florentine Renaissance art. Though here in Florence, thought Georgia as she joined the queue waiting to get in, she really should think of it as the

Rinascimento, since she was in the place where it all
began.

Surrounded by tourists and students talking every
language under the sun, Georgia waited patiently,
watching the waiters who moved among the tables in
the outdoor restaurants. She would have dearly liked
a cappuccino, but not enough to yield her place in a
line which was already snaking in a double row as the
time to open approached.

At last Georgia paid her lire and ascended the great
stone Vasari staircase to the gallery where the
paintings, she found, were arranged by centuries, so
that the art lover could feed on a banquet of art laid
out in strict chronological order from the thirteenth
to the eighteenth century.

If the outing had been planned as a welcome diversion to take her mind off Luca Valori, it failed.
As Georgia moved from one famous painting to
another she found her delight in the visual feast
marred by a quite violent longing to have him beside
her to share it. She had managed to persuade herself
these past few days that she'd done rather well in ex-
pelling him from her life. It was daunting to find
herself so wrong.

But her depression lifted gradually as Georgia,
daughter of a surveyor, gazed on paintings which displayed the Renaissance skill and fascination with perspective. And the exquisite paganism of the maidens
in Botticelli's *Primavera*, when she managed to find
space enough in the crowd to gaze at them, was just
as enchanting as she'd expected.

It was a couple of hours later, feeling almost dazed
by such an overdose of visual pleasure, that Georgia
emerged from the gallery near the Loggia dei Lanzi,

and managed to find a free table in a crowded outdoor café. She ordered a much needed cappuccino and a pastry, and settled down to write the postcards she'd bought in the Uffizi, deeply remorseful at posting James her goodbye letter instead of the views of Florence sent to her parents and Charlotte and Tom.

She sighed and ordered another cappuccino then went off to tackle the wait to get into the Bargello, which her guidebook stated had once been the prison where the bell tolled for every execution. These days, she read, it was to sculpture what the Uffizi was to paintings.

Georgia paid her bill, then threaded her way through the crowd, past the great square fortress of the Palazzo Vecchio with its high off-centre tower, and with the aid of her map quickly reached the Bargello to see the great achievements of Michelangelo and Donatello, who'd lived to be eighty, she read as she waited in line, and was never short of commissions. When Georgia finally saw the latter's long-haired *David* in bronze in the Great Hall on the first floor she could see why.

The Bargello was about to close by the time she'd paid the various works of Michelangelo and his contemporaries the necessary respect. Her ankle had begun to throb, her head ached a little, and Georgia decided to skip lunch and call it a day.

She caught a train back as soon as she got to the station, and abandoned any idea of ringing Franco to fetch her, as arranged. She was much earlier than intended, and Franco might not even be there, which might force Marco Sardi to collect her. For once, she thought, yawning in the crowded train, she would forget the expense and take a taxi from Lucca to the villa.

When Georgia finally arrived at the house she found it in uproar. Alessa came running to her and flung herself into Georgia's arms, crying bitterly, followed by a distraught Pina.

'It is the master,' said Pina, red-eyed. 'He has been taken ill. Signor Luca has driven him to the hospital.'

'Hospital?' asked Georgia, going cold. Her arms tightened round Alessa. 'There, there, darling, don't cry so hard.'

'Papa's ill!' sobbed Alessa, and looked up at Georgia in appeal. 'Will he go to heaven like Mamma?'

'Of course not, darling,' said Georgia firmly, devoutly hoping that she was right.

'But Papa had a pain and Dr Fassi said he must go to the hospital so they could make the pain go away.' The child burrowed her head into Georgia's shoulder. 'Dr Fassi made your pain go away here, at home!'

'I think you should let Pina wash your face, while I go and talk to Elsa,' said Georgia lovingly. 'Then perhaps you and I could have tea together in the conservatory, darling.'

With utmost reluctance Alessa went upstairs with Pina while Georgia raced to the kitchen to talk with Elsa.

'It looked like a heart attack,' said the housekeeper, confirming Georgia's worst fears. She sighed, her face lined with worry. 'Thank the good Lord you came back early. Fortunately Signor Luca was here and took charge.'

'I should have been here,' said Georgia wretchedly. 'I could have gone to Florence any time. Signor Sardi insisted I took time off, but—'

'My dear, you're here now.' Elsa managed a smile as Alessa came back with Pina. 'Now you shall have some tea—perhaps something to eat. Are you hungry?'

Georgia shook her head and put an arm round the little girl. 'Just some tea, and perhaps some of your delicious biscuits, Elsa. Come on, darling.'

As soon as they reached the conservatory Alessa climbed onto Georgia's lap. 'I want to see Papa,' she said forlornly.

'The moment the doctor says you can, you shall,' promised Georgia, and coaxed her to eat some of the biscuits that Elsa brought in herself with the tea, Pina following close behind.

'It is good you are back,' said Elsa, watching the child relax in Georgia's arms.

'I'll move back upstairs, next to Alessa,' said Georgia with decision, and Pina hurried off to move Georgia's belongings, plainly glad to have occupation.

Alessa, worn out with tears and shock, was already half-asleep against Georgia's shoulder as Elsa confided in an undertone that she had been worried about the master for some time.

'So have I,' agreed Georgia softly, smoothing the child's ruffled dark curls. 'He's eaten very little for the past week or two.'

Elsa nodded, looking worried. 'Thank God Luca was here. He is a tower of strength in emergency.' She gave Georgia a wry little smile. 'The only time I've seen him lose his head was the night he came in with you unconscious in his arms.'

Georgia flushed, but met the woman's eyes squarely. 'He will move back here now, of course.'

Elsa nodded. 'He has no choice. Alessa needs him.'

So do I, thought Georgia. 'Elsa,' she said quickly, 'does Signora Valori know?'

The woman shook her head. 'She is old. Signor Luca thought it best to wait a little until—'

'Until you have better news to give her,' said Georgia firmly, shifting the sleeping child more comfortably on her lap.

Elsa nodded, brightening. 'True. Now I shall take away the tray and make a start on dinner.'

Alessa slept for a while, then woke with a start. The relief on her face when she found herself with Georgia was deeply moving, and won her a hug and a kiss.

'Papa?' said the child hopefully.

'No news yet, poppet,' said Georgia, getting to her feet. She held out her hand to the child. 'Come on, let's find Pina and get you bathed and in your nightgown. Then I'll read to you, and as a treat maybe you can have a snack in bed for once.'

The programme met with tearful approval and Alessa went off with Georgia obediently, calling for Pina as they went through the hall. Bathtime was as protracted and time-consuming as Georgia could make it, made joyful in the end when a panting Elsa burst in, beaming all over her face.

'Signor Luca has telephoned to say your Papa is better, little one. He sends his love and tells you to be a good girl.'

The joy on Alessa's face was so radiant that Georgia had to swallow hard.

'Now I am hungry!' announced Alessa, and Elsa took Pina off at once, promising to send her up with a special supper by way of celebration.

It was after nine by the time Alessa was sleeping peacefully and Georgia felt free to take a swift bath. Surprised to realise that she was hungry too, she brushed her hair dry as quickly as possible, dressed swiftly in the almond-pink dress and went to check on Alessa. By the light of a small lamp she found the child fast asleep and Pina dozing in a chair beside the bed. Relieved, she went downstairs to find Elsa crossing the hall.

'I will bring dinner to the conservatory in a few minutes,' said the woman, plainly in a hurry to get back to the kitchen, and Georgia, armed with a book, went along the corridor to the conservatory, happy to read for a while until the meal arrived.

But Luca Valori had arrived before her. He rose to his feet, elegant as always, but his face weary below hair still damp from a shower.

'Elsa tells me you know I must stay here while Marco is in hospital,' he said without preliminaries. 'I have no choice.'

'But of course!' Georgia bit her lip. 'I had no right to ask you to go. Not that any of that is the least important now. How is Signor Sardi?'

Luca pulled out a chair for her and resumed his own. 'He is better. It was not a heart attack, as we all feared. He was in great pain, but it was due to what the consultant in Pisa diagnosed as an inflamed gullet, not a problem with his heart.'

Georgia let out a great sigh of relief. 'Thank heavens! I know all about that, as it happens. My father suffered from it a year or so back before he retired. It's the preliminary stage to—to—' She searched for the word and Luca smiled.

'Ulcers,' he supplied. 'Brought on by stress, of which Marco has had more than his share since Maddalena died.'

Georgia gave him a smile of such radiant relief that his eyes lit in swift response.

'He was obliged to swallow a camera!' he said, grimacing, and Georgia nodded.

'I don't know what you call it, but in English it's an endoscopy. My father had that done. It highlights the problem and shows it up on a television screen. In Dad's case it meant a careful diet and a course of pills and medicine, and now, unless he's careless, he has no problem at all.'

'Good. I trust it will be the same for Marco—' Luca leapt to his feet suddenly. 'Forgive me, I did not offer you a drink. I thought we might celebrate with champagne.'

'I ought to eat something before I have a drink,' said Georgia apologetically. 'Since breakfast two cappuccinos are all I've had all day except some tea when I came home.'

Luca gave her a sharp look, then smiled slowly. 'I'm glad.'

'That I haven't eaten anything?'

He shook his head. 'That you can think of the Villa Toscana as home—in the circumstances.'

CHAPTER NINE

OVER dinner that night Georgia did her best to keep the atmosphere light, and in the main Luca co-operated. In their mutual relief that Marco Sardi's illness was not a heart attack after all, they ate an excellent dinner of Elsa's famed *bistecca fiorentina,* accompanied by a Chianti Classico of such excellence that Georgia rashly cast caution to the winds and drank two glasses of it as well as the celebratory glass of vintage champagne.

During the meal they discussed the paintings and sculpture that Georgia had seen earlier, the redecoration in train at Luca's house in the hills and the new orders crowding in for the Supremo, talking together like two civilised people as though the incident in the ground-floor bedroom had never happened.

As they drank coffee together later Luca smiled at Georgia teasingly.

'So you have been to Florence without seeing Michelangelo's *David*!'

Georgia nodded ruefully. 'I left him for the crowning touch to the day, but after the visit to the Bargello I was tired and my ankle hurt, so I caught the next train back instead.'

'It must have been a shock to arrive home to the news of Marco.'

'It was.' She shivered. 'Poor little Alessa was in a terrible state, convinced he was going to die like her mamma.'

He stared into his cup, his eyes sombre. 'He was in such pain that I confess I shared her fears.' He looked up with a smile. 'They were unfounded, thank God, and we can all sleep in peace tonight.'

Georgia nodded. 'And I shall hear if Alessa wakes.'

'Then you have moved back to the room next to hers,' he said, with a scowl.

'Yes.'

'You could not bear to stay in the other one?'

She eyed his averted profile with hostility. 'Nothing of the sort. On Dr Fassi's advice I did stay there until today. But I thought I'd sleep near Alessa in the circumstances, in case she might need me in the night.'

'It is a coincidence, then, that you moved once you knew I was coming back to the villa to stay?'

'Entirely.'

He lifted a sardonic eyebrow, and thrust out his cup for more coffee.

Georgia refilled it with a commendably steady hand. 'Should you drink so much coffee late at night?'

'I sleep badly lately whether I drink coffee or not,' he said with sudden violence, and drained the cup.

Georgia rose to her feet hurriedly. 'It's late—time I went to bed. Goodnight. I'm glad Signor Sardi is not in danger.'

Luca stood up, looking down at her broodingly. 'I shall take Alessa to Pisa to visit him tomorrow. Take advantage of her absence and rest, Georgia. You look tired.'

'It's been quite a day,' she returned lightly.

'Very true.' He gave her a formal little bow. 'Goodnight. I think it best I deny myself the pleasure of escorting you to your room.'

She bit her lip, then on impulse held out her hand. 'Luca, couldn't we forget everything that happened before today? Go on from here as—as friends for the rest of my stay, for Alessa's sake?'

He lifted her hand to his lips and kissed it. 'Very well, Georgia. If that is what you wish.' He smiled into her eyes. 'Only a fool would refuse friendship offered by a beautiful woman. And I may be many things but I am not a fool.' His mouth twisted. 'Except on a certain recent occasion, of course.'

Georgia withdrew her hand. 'I repeat, Luca, let's forget all that. Goodnight.'

Next morning Luca was waiting at the breakfast table when Georgia arrived with Alessa. He brought a beaming smile to the child's face by telling her that he'd rung the hospital, that Papa was much better and looking forward to her visit that afternoon.

Alessa was so overjoyed that the meal was a very happy one, with no constraint possible between the two adults as the child chattered nineteen to the dozen. Later all three of them spent time in the pool, and afterwards shared a cold lunch in the garden.

'Luca says you must rest while we are away this afternoon,' ordered Alessa, and Georgia smiled.

'Then of course I will,' she said demurely, and Luca laughed.

'Because you feel inclined to do so, no doubt, not from any obedience to my wishes!'

'You understand me very well,' she said as Alessa went off with Pina to tidy herself for the outing.

'If only that were true!'

'I'm a very uncomplicated person.'

'So am I.'

'In that case life should be peaceful for the rest of my stay.'

'It is a possibility, of course.' Luca smiled. 'But I think you should know that I meant every word, Georgia.'

She fixed him with a dark, suspicious gaze. 'Which word in particular?'

'I am merely making it clear that although I have agreed to this friendship you propose I still want to be your lover. Even more now than before.'

Georgia frowned. 'What do you mean?'

He stared at her, swinging car keys from a long, slim forefinger. 'I am obsessed with the desire to teach you the full glory of what love can be between a man and a woman.' His eyes kindled. 'I found your surprising lack of expertise in such circumstances very seductive. I yearn to further your education, English teacher. It is *that*, not the coffee, which keeps me awake at night.'

A great tide of colour rushed into her face, her angry retort stifled by the return of Alessa in all the glory of a new blue dress.

'I'm ready, I'm ready,' cried the child, running towards them. She held up her face for Georgia's kiss, then took Luca by the hand. 'See you later, Georgia.'

'Yes, darling,' said Georgia with difficulty. 'My best wishes to your father.'

Luca smiled at Georgia, his eyes brilliant with laughter at her barely contained outrage. 'Make sure you rest,' he said softly, with such false solicitude that her teeth ground together as he took his little niece off to the waiting car.

Left to herself, Georgia lay in a garden chair under an umbrella, in no mood to take herself off to bed as

Elsa strongly advised. She needed to be in the open air, too restless to cage herself up in her room after Luca's parting shot. In a way, she conceded when she'd calmed down a little, it was flattering that he still wanted to make love to her after the embarrassing sequel to the first time. But that was it, of course—a simple matter of image. Gianluca Valori wanted her to remember him as the greatest lover of all time. Which, unfortunately, he was, as far as she was concerned.

Not that it mattered, Georgia promised herself. No way would it happen again. And not solely because it would be incredibly stupid on her part either. She found Luca Valori irresistible in almost every way, and she'd be lying to herself if she tried to deny it. His kisses and caresses set her on fire as no other man's had ever come near to doing. Georgia's heart beat faster and her pulse raced at the mere thought of his lovemaking and she buried herself in her book, forcing her attention on the story in an attempt to erase him from her mind.

When Pina brought a tea-tray out later she reported that Signor Luca had rung to say that he would be later than expected in returning because he was taking Alessa to her aunt's house near Lucca on the way home, to report to Signor Sardi's sister.

Georgia was glad of the respite. She had a leisurely swim as the heat lessened, then went indoors to laze in the bath and finish her book before making her weekly call to her parents. After talking to her mother she felt restless and a little homesick as usual, and, to get over it, spent a lot of time fussing with her hair and going through her limited wardrobe for something to wear to dinner. Although she refused to become Luca Valori's latest playmate, she was human enough to want to look her best for the meal that they would share alone in Marco Sardi's absence.

But Franco was obliged to fetch Alessa home from her aunt's house. Luca had been called away to some crisis at Valorino.

On a Sunday evening? A likely story, thought Georgia scathingly as she listened to Alessa's account of her visit to the hospital. No doubt he had a very different kind of call to make, on some lady more complaisant than Alessa's English teacher.

'The doctor says Papa needs rest,' reported Alessa, 'so he must stay at the hospital for a little while. But he is much better, Georgia. Oh, I forgot. Zia Claudia said I must tell you she was sorry not to bring me home herself. She drove to Pisa to see Papa instead.'

Having taken such care with her appearance, Georgia couldn't bring herself to plead a headache and ask Elsa for a tray in her room. Once Alessa was settled for the night Georgia was obliged to eat in solitary splendour in the conservatory, her dinner utterly ruined by speculation on where Luca was eating his, and with whom.

Furious at her irrational jealousy, Georgia forced herself to linger with the tea-tray that Elsa insisted on providing, then went for a stroll in the garden before taking herself to bed. As she wandered restlessly under the velvety, starlit sky she heard a car turn in at the gate and her heart leapt as she recognised the distinctive throaty growl of the Supremo.

Luca was a lot earlier than expected. Georgia hurried into the house, then slowed deliberately to a walk on her way to the hall, where she found Luca on his way to the stairs. To her astonishment he was filthy.

'There *was* a crisis, then?' she said, and could have bitten her tongue at the gleam of white teeth in Luca's dirty face.

'You doubted it?' he said mockingly.

Georgia shrugged. 'On a Sunday night it seemed—unusual.'

'There was a fire in one of the outbuildings at the *fabbrica*. Nothing serious. I helped put it out,' he said without drama.

'No fire brigade?'

'Oh, yes, they came. But by that time the flames were under control—we are prepared for such accidents.' He scowled. 'Someone disregarded the "no smoking" signs.'

Elsa came hurrying into the hall, and gave a screech at the sight of him. 'Luca! What happened?'

He explained, and she went hurrying off to prepare a meal, telling him to get out of his filthy clothes at once and take a bath.

Luca smiled wryly. 'You must find my relationship with our servants strange.'

'No.' Georgia grinned. 'We don't have any at home to have a relationship with.'

'Elsa was with the family before I was born. She is fiercely independent in many ways, yet her loyalty to us all is unswerving, always.'

'Just as well, when you come home at this hour on a Sunday night expecting dinner!'

'It would be useless to tell her not to bother. Besides,' added Luca, 'I am starving. Forgive me, I must take a shower.' Halfway to the stairs he turned. 'Will you stay to talk to me while I eat? Or are you too tired?'

Georgia knew she could easily say that she'd been on her way to bed. But in two weeks' time she would be saying goodbye to Luca Valori for good. 'No,' she said before she could change her mind.

'No, you will not stay, or no, you are not too tired?'

'I'm not tired,' she said with perfect truth. 'If you want I'll keep you company.'

'Thank you,' he said gravely. 'I will be ten minutes.'

Georgia watched him leaping up the stairs, then turned to make her way back to the conservatory, feeling pensive. She might not want a love affair with Luca Valori, but it was very hard to refuse herself the pleasure of his company while she still had the chance.

Luca, hair still wet, joined her in less than ten minutes, and downed a large quantity of mineral water before he allowed himself a glass of wine. 'It was thirsty work tonight, but no harm done, thank God. No one was hurt.'

'You feel great responsibility for your employees, I take it,' said Georgia.

'Our workforce is not very big, and most of them have been with us for years and send their sons for training to take their places.' Luca smiled. 'Naturally I feel responsible, as my father did before me. Sadly he died when I was in school, so it was left to Maddalena to take responsibility until I was of an age to do so myself.'

'And your mother?' said Georgia hesitantly. 'I don't wish to pry, but did she die young too?'

'At my birth,' he said tersely. 'As did Maddalena when her son was born.'

Georgia looked stricken. 'I'm so sorry—I shouldn't have asked!'

'Why not? It is no secret.' Luca looked up in relief as Elsa came in with a laden tray. 'Wonderful. I could eat a horse.'

'You will eat veal and artichokes, as Georgia did. A good thing I kept some back for you,' said Elsa severely. 'Why can't you leave the dirty work to others, Luca?'

'Because I like it too much,' he said, seizing a knife and fork. 'Now leave me in peace to eat, woman. I'm too old for your scolding.'

Elsa snorted, directed a look of pure love at his sleek dark head and went back to fetch more tea for Georgia.

'Do you never tire of all this tea?' demanded Luca, his mouth full, and Georgia giggled.

'Actually I do, sometimes, but Elsa is convinced the British drink nothing else, so I haven't the heart to disillusion her. Tell me,' she added, 'is Signor Sardi really well enough to leave hospital soon, as Alessa said?'

Luca assured her that after a few days' complete rest, which Marco was already bored with, he would be fit enough to come home. 'Along with a course of medication and a strict diet for a while, just as you said. No wine or spirits, no coffee, no vinegar in salad dressings, no citrus fruits.'

Georgia nodded. 'Nothing to aggravate acidity.'

Luca pulled a face. 'I pity him. Marco loves wine and coffee with equal passion. However, as I pointed out to him, it will be worth it to spare Alessa another fright like that. It was a powerful argument.'

When Luca had finished his meal he proposed a walk in the gardens. 'To clear the smoke from my lungs,' he said, coughing a little.

Georgia went with him gladly. 'The stars here look so enormous,' she commented as they strolled across the manicured grass.

'It is more southerly here than your country, Georgia.' Luca breathed in deeply. 'At my house it is cooler, because it is higher up in the hills. Will you visit me there before you leave, Georgia? Bring Alessa to chaperon if you wish!'

'Then I will. Is the work nearly finished there?'

He shrugged. 'It was only a few repairs to a wall, and a new coat of paint in my bedroom. It is very different from this house. Not so civilised. It was a farm once. I want to preserve its identity.'

'It sounds interesting. Charlotte and Tom stayed at a farmhouse somewhere...' Georgia trailed into silence, wishing that she'd had the sense to keep quiet on the subject, and Luca caught her by the arm, bringing her to a halt beyond the shrubbery which lined the lawns near the house. The trout stream rushed by, giving its illusion of coolness, and Georgia stood very still, conscious in every nerve of the heat in Luca's hand, of the scent of grass and flowers in the air, of the knowledge that this moment would never come again.

'Tell me that you are not in love with this James of yours,' commanded Luca abruptly, and Georgia sighed, unable to lie.

'I suppose I'm not,' she admitted reluctantly. 'At least, not in the way that you mean.'

'There is only one way,' he whispered. 'This way.' He drew her into his arms and kissed her, and Georgia yielded to the pressure of a long hand at her waist as he slid the other into her hair to hold her face still. Luca's mouth settled on hers with a coaxing delicacy that seduced her far more effectively than a bruising kiss of passion. With a sigh she slid her arms round his neck and felt a tremor run through the body that felt so natural, so utterly right against her own. The quality of the kiss altered and their breathing quickened, and suddenly his arms were cracking her ribs and her fingers were digging into his shoulders, and with a muffled sound he buried his face against her hair.

'I want you, Georgia,' he said, so quietly that she sensed his words rather than heard them.

'I know.'

'Do you want me?'

She was so long in answering that he raised his head and put a finger under her chin to lift her face to his. 'Is your silence my answer?' he demanded. 'Are you telling me you feel nothing for me, when I know very well that you do? I *know* when a woman trembles to my touch, when her lips open to me like a flower—'

'Yes, I know you know,' she said flatly. 'And that's the trouble.'

'Trouble?' He thrust her away from him to stare down at her in the dim light. 'I cannot read your face out here in the dark,' he said, and tightened his grip on her arms. 'What do you mean?'

'You know far too much about women. Which isn't surprising with your looks and reputation—'

'Reputation?' he demanded, incensed.

'As a racing driver,' Georgia said quickly. 'You must have had lots of adulation in your time, Gianluca Valori. And a great many women must have wanted you, for your looks, for your body, and for something else that some men have and some men don't—charisma, sex appeal, call it what you like.'

'Whatever it is, you are obviously immune to it,' he said bitterly, and dropped his hands.

'No, I'm not,' she sighed. 'I wish I was. But in a fortnight I'll be gone from here, and soon after that I'm returning to my job at the school near Venice.' Suddenly she reverted to English, needing the exact words to hammer home her point. 'You can't be my lover for the simple reason that, even if there were no James and I was willing, here in Italy you're too well-known. I'd lose my job if I became another of your playmates, Luca.'

'Playmates?' he said with distaste.

'Whatever you like to call your ladies,' she said bluntly. 'I'm not denying that I find you attractive. Out here under these big Italian stars of yours I'd have to be a nun not to respond to you. But I'm not going to because you and I inhabit different worlds. I'm not getting involved with you, Luca. You agreed to be friends, remember. Are you going back on your word?'

Luca breathed in deeply, shaking his head. 'No,' he said wearily. 'I will not go back on my word. You win, Georgia. If it is friendship you want, then I shall never touch you again.' He thrust a hand through his hair. 'And I shall keep to it because just to touch you drives me mad. I have never wanted a woman the way I desire you.'

'Only because you can't have me, Luca,' she said gently, and turned away and went back alone through the gardens, wincing at the glare of the security lights as she broke into a run in her hurry to get in the house.

Breathless and oddly desolate, she snatched up her book and hurried up the stairs to her room, haunted by the feeling that she'd just made some fateful, irreparable mistake.

CHAPTER TEN

GEORGIA saw very little of Luca after that. Due to
Marco's absence from the *fabbrica* Luca spent so
much time there that sometimes a brief half-hour in
the late evening was all the contact they had. There
were no more dinners for two, nor moonlit strolls in
the garden. Which made things easier all round,
Georgia told herself firmly. And when Marco Sardi
came home there were only a few days left of her stay
at the Villa Toscana.

Luca drove Marco to the villa during the afternoon, stayed for a while at Alessa's request, then returned to Valorino with nothing more personal for
Georgia than his white, public smile in farewell.

Marco Sardi looked so much better that Alessa was
ecstatic, and pleaded to stay up for the evening meal
as a special treat. Her father consented indulgently,
telling her that Signora Valori would be joining them.

'She likes to eat early, so it will suit everyone,' he
declared. 'Other than Luca, of course, who likes to
eat late. But he will not be joining us tonight. He is
attending a business dinner in my place, as represen-
tative of Fabbrica Valori.'

Georgia went off to help Alessa choose a dress to
wear for dinner, feeling tense. The prospect of Signora
Valori at the dinner table was daunting, particularly
since Luca would be absent from it.

When Georgia was dressing Pina knocked at the
door to say that Signor Marco would like a word with

her in his study before dinner. Georgia tied back her hair with a black velvet ribbon, tucked her cream silk shirt into the waistband of her narrow black linen skirt, then went downstairs. She knocked at the study door and went in, a questioning smile on her face.

'You wished to see me, Signor Sardi?'

He was dressed informally, in a light linen suit with a silk shirt open at the collar, and looked rested and a lot younger after his enforced rest in hospital. He smiled at her and waved her to a seat in front of his desk, then took the chair behind it.

'Georgia, I wish to thank you for all your good services to Alessa. Knowing she had you, as well as Elsa and Pina, made my time in hospital easier to bear.'

'You're very kind,' murmured Georgia.

Marco Sardi regarded her with speculation. 'And now I'm going to presume on *your* kindness and ask a great favour.'

'If I can help in any way I'll be glad to,' she said promptly.

'Would you consider prolonging your stay?' He smiled wryly. 'If you would stay here with us until Alessa goes back to school I would be deeply grateful.'

'But I thought you were leaving for England at the end of August,' she said, surprised.

'My doctors have forbidden that for the time being. The opening of the London office has been postponed until the New Year.'

'I see.' Georgia looked down at her clasped hands. 'I had rather hoped to spend time with my parents—'

'Of course, of course.' His smile was kind. 'Since my doctor says I may not return to the *fabbrica* for a few days, why not fly home this weekend to visit your family? I have already contacted Signora Blanchard at the school in Venice, and she gives you leave for the first week of term, so that you may visit your parents again before you begin the new academic year.' Marco Sardi smiled in wry apology. 'I thought it best to gain official permission before laying my plan before you.'

Georgia hadn't the heart to refuse. 'Then, yes. If you really want me to I'll stay.'

He rose to his feet, holding out his hand. 'You have my grateful thanks, Georgia. Now join us in the conservatory. Emilia has already arrived.'

The meeting with Signora Valori passed off with no awkwardness at all, to Georgia's relief. Elsa surpassed herself with the meal, and Alessa's joy in having her father home invested the evening with an air of festivity not even Luca's absence could spoil.

'Alessa has been talking to me in English,' observed the elegant old lady in approval. 'I am not fluent in your language, Georgia, but speak enough to know Alessa has made splendid progress.'

'Thank you, *signora*.' Georgia smiled at the little girl. 'We work well together, don't we, poppet?'

Alessa nodded happily. 'Lessons with Georgia are fun!'

'Then you will be pleased to know Georgia has consented to stay with us until you return to school,' said her father, and Alessa's eyes opened wide in delight.

'You will really stay, Georgia?'

Georgia nodded, any doubts about the idea not only dispelled by the child's reaction, but by Signora Valori's approval later. After Alessa went to bed the two women were left together while Marco strolled in the garden to smoke the one cigar a day that he was allowed.

'It is good to see the child so happy, Georgia. You are kind to give up more of your time.'

'It's not exactly a hardship to stay on in this beautiful house to teach a bright little pupil like Alessa,' said Georgia with truth.

'I know, my dear.' The astute blue eyes locked with Georgia's. 'But after the incident with Luca—which it is better to discuss than leave festering in secret—I thought perhaps you would have wished to leave the moment your time here was over.'

Georgia's eyes never wavered. 'There was no real harm done, *signora*. As I said at the time, it was a misunderstanding. Which has been cleared up. Luca and I have agreed to be friends.'

'Friends?' said Emilia Valori drily. 'Luca has really agreed to this?'

Georgia smiled rather mischievously. 'More or less.'

'In my experience, my dear, pure friendship is surprisingly difficult between a beautiful woman and a red-blooded man. If only on one side there is usually a desire for something warmer eventually.' The blue eyes twinkled. 'You feel no desire at all for my grandson?'

'Of course I do.' Georgia smiled ruefully. 'But I have no intention of giving in to it. There are too many differences between us. Background, culture—all kinds of things.'

'Including religion, I imagine,' said the old lady thoughtfully.

'Actually, no. I'm not as devout as my parents would like, but I'm a Catholic just the same.'

'I see. Does Luca know this?'

'No. I've seen no reason to tell him—or anyone else except you, *signora*.'

'Because respect for my great age forbids you to tell me to mind my own business!' The old lady laughed, and Marco strolled in to join them, pleased to see them enjoying each other's company.

Georgia enjoyed her brief holiday at home. The time passed swiftly, though Georgia did little more than walk the dog, help her mother with the cooking, do a little weeding with her father and stay in bed late each morning to make up for her irritating insomnia at night.

Charlotte and Tom joined them for Sunday lunch, which meant a lot of good-natured teasing about the hostile Italian, but the subject was dropped the moment Charlotte, beaming, informed her family that she was pregnant.

'It wasn't a stomach upset at all!' she said as Georgia hugged her. 'I rather suspected as much, but I wouldn't say a word in case I was mistaken.'

Georgia turned to Tom, laughing. 'So it's all your fault, then.'

He grinned like a Cheshire cat. 'It had better be!'

The parting from her family was surprisingly hard when the time came to leave them at Heathrow. If it hadn't been for Alessa Georgia would have got back in the car and given up all thought of ever returning to the Villa Toscana, and thus stayed safely out of Luca's orbit for good. She would have avoided mentioning him to her parents at all if her father hadn't discovered, via Tom, that he was actually Gianluca

Valori, well-known to fans of Formula-One Grand Prix racing.

'We shan't see you now until September, then,' said her mother, hugging her, and Georgia nodded, feeling oddly tearful.

'I'll come home for a week before I start school,' she promised, and tore herself away to go through to the flight-departure lounge to wait for the plane to Pisa. This time Franco would be waiting for her at the airport with the car, instead of her having to take the train to Florence.

When the plane landed Georgia collected her luggage, made her way through Customs then stopped dead, her pulse racing as she saw a familiar dark head above the crowd.

Luca craned his neck, then his eyes met hers, lit up, and he pushed his way towards her and took her bag. 'Welcome back, Georgia. I had business in Pisa, so I relieved Franco of the task of meeting you. You enjoyed your weekend?'

'Yes,' she said breathlessly, appalled by how pleased she was to see him. 'So much I almost didn't come back.'

Luca frowned as they went to the car park. 'You did not wish to return to us?'

'Yes, of course. I wouldn't hurt Alessa for the world—'

'But you had no care for my feelings!' he threw at her, and unlocked the gleaming black Supremo. He tossed her bag in the back, then helped her into the passenger seat and got in behind the wheel. He turned to look at her, and Georgia swallowed, suddenly overcome by the sheer force of his physical presence in the confines of the car.

She could see the faint blue shadow along his newly shaved jaw, smell the faint citrus scent of something he'd used afterwards, and as he flung a familiar suede jacket onto the back seat his hand brushed against her shoulder and the contact sent a stab of fire through her. So much for friendship, she thought bitterly as he started the engine. Her instincts had been right. She should never have come back.

They chatted politely, like two acquaintances, until they reached the road to the villa, then Luca turned a molten sidelong look on her. 'I missed you, Georgia.'

'But you're hardly ever at home!'

'Then you missed me also,' he stated in triumph, grinning through the windscreen.

'Of course. Everyone at Villa Toscana misses you when you're not there,' she said prosaically, but Luca's grin only widened as he turned the car into the familiar driveway.

Georgia had barely time to get out of the car before a small figure came hurtling from the house into her arms, hugging her in a frenzy of delighted welcome, crying her name over and over again, and Georgia knew that if only for Alessa's sake she'd had no choice about coming back.

Alessa clutched her hand as the three of them went into the house, and said in triumphant, careful English, 'Welcome home, Georgia. I have missed you very much.'

'What a clever girl!' crowed Georgia, and entered the hall to such enthusiastic greetings from Elsa and Pina that she could have been away for five years instead of five days—a comment made with dry amusement by Marco Sardi as he came strolling from the study to add to Georgia's welcome.

Georgia dismissed her qualms as she dressed for dinner that evening, deciding that now she was back she would take each day as it came and enjoy it to the full—something to look back on with pleasure when she left the villa for good to get on with the rest of her life. Fine words, she told her reflection drily, now you're here. But afterwards you may feel different, my girl.

It was good to dine in company with the two men again, to laugh at Marco Sardi's grumbling when Elsa served a dinner tailored to his new diet rather than to his preferences. Georgia listened with avidity as the two men discussed the latest political crisis, and contributed her own account of the televised Puccini opera seen during her stay at home.

'Your family is well?' enquired Marco, and Georgia nodded.

'Very well; particularly my sister. We all had lunch together on Sunday, and Charlotte announced she is expecting a baby—' She bit her lip, and Marco shook his head at her reassuringly.

'Georgia, life goes on and babies arrive. I trust your brother-in-law is very happy at the news?'

Georgia nodded, avoiding Luca's eyes. 'So is my mother!'

After dinner Marco excused himself to retire to bed early.

'I am still under orders, you understand,' he said wryly. 'Luca is a stern taskmaster. He says I may not return to Valorino if I break the rules.'

Luca nodded, grinning. 'I promised Dr Fassi I would make you keep to your diet and get plenty of rest. So goodnight, Marco; sleep well.'

'The weather has broken,' said Luca after he'd gone. 'So tonight there is no walk in the garden. Sit here with me for a while. It is too early to go to bed.'

Georgia curled up in the corner of a sofa, listening to the rain drumming on the glass roof. For a moment Luca stood looking at her, as though he took pleasure at the mere sight of her, then he sat beside her, took her hand and looked into her eyes.

'Does it trouble you, this baby of your sister's?'

Oddly enough, it did in a way, thought Georgia, but only because she felt a totally surprising envy. At the memory of Tom's euphoria she smiled involuntarily.

'Not in the least,' she said cheerfully. 'Charlotte was quite ill when we first arrived in Florence. I'm only too pleased that her stomach upset was due to nothing more serious than pregnancy.'

Luca's fingers smoothed the back of her hand delicately. 'I hope all goes well with her.'

'There's no reason why it shouldn't,' said Georgia, surprised.

'It is not always so.' He gave her a sombre look. 'Have you never wondered why I am not married?'

'Often.'

'Because, if I marry, everyone will expect a Valori heir to carry on the name.' His grasp tightened cruelly. 'You know what happened to my mother and Maddalena. I will put no woman at such risk.'

Georgia gazed at him, astonished. 'But surely you want a family of your own?'

'I have Alessa.' His eyes lit with a glow which rang alarm bells in Georgia's brain. 'And I have no intention of denying myself the pleasures that all men crave. I need *you*, Georgia. I invented the appointment in Pisa today just so that I could meet your plane. Because I could not endure another moment without you. Can you look at me with those beautiful black eyes and tell me that you care nothing for me?'

'No,' she said baldly, 'I can't.'

'Then why must we keep to this ludicrous idea of friendship?' he said hoarsely. 'I would not offend your principles by suggesting you share my bed here in Marco's house. But I have a house of my own—'

'Are you suggesting we sneak off at weekends to your place?' she demanded, incensed.

'No!' He caught the hands she wrenched away. 'Listen, Georgia. Do not go back to the school in Venice. Come to me at the farm—'

'Why?' she demanded scornfully. 'You don't need English lessons.'

'No. I need *this*.' Luca caught her in his arms and kissed her, but she twisted away.

'I knew I shouldn't have come back,' she said bitterly, and jumped to her feet, but Luca leapt to bar her way.

'Why?' he demanded, his eyes glittering into hers. 'You wished to stay with this James of yours, who writes to you so much? He was there, in England?'

'No. I told you—he's in Cyprus,' she said wearily. 'I didn't see him.'

'Good!' Luca relaxed, a look in his eyes that, with wrath, she identified as satisfaction. 'It is no use to fight, Georgia. We were meant to be lovers. You know it.'

'I know nothing of the kind.' Georgia pushed him aside, but he caught her in his arms, holding her close. She stiffened, but Luca shook his head.

'It is no use,' he repeated softly. 'Your body tells me what you refuse to admit.'

'Possibly,' she said hotly. 'You're a very sexy man, and I'm a normal, healthy female, but that's as far as it goes. When I leave here we'll never—'

The rest of her protest was smothered by his mouth, which took possession of hers with such flagrant ownership that she thrust at him with impotent hands, only to have them caught in one of his as he raised his head to look down into her eyes.

'Never is a long time,' he whispered. 'In the night I wake thinking of how you felt beneath me that day, of the silken feel of your skin...'

Georgia tried to close her ears to the deep voice which whispered such liquid, mellifluous seduction that her traitorous body responded to it even as her brain told her to drag herself away while she still could. Her breathing grew ragged and chills ran down her spine as he slid his mouth to her throat, then she pulled herself together and pushed him away, meeting the heat in his eyes with a look so bright and cold that he scowled blackly.

'What is it?'

'Luca, listen to me. I'm not going to live with you. If—if there were no James, perhaps if you were someone more—more ordinary, my own nationality, even, I might consider it. With you it's different.'

He stood back, his face suddenly hard. 'You mean I must marry you before I am granted the delights of your bed?'

'Good heavens, no,' she said, so genuinely surprised that she spoke in English. 'It never occurred to me.'

'I find that very hard to believe,' he replied silkily, in accented, but perfectly plain English. 'Are you saying that if I asked you to be my wife you would refuse?' He shook his head, smiling cynically. 'I do not think so.'

'You must believe what you choose, of course,' she said very quietly, 'but it's the truth. I don't want to marry you, or anyone else at this particular moment in time. Not even James. I like my life the way it is. And James is willing to wait until I'm ready to settle down.'

'You are lucky to have so tame a lover,' sneered Luca, a pulse throbbing beside his set mouth. 'If you were mine—'

'But I'm not,' she said coolly. 'Goodnight.'

Georgia arrived in her room a few moments later, feeling so weary that she could have scaled the north face of the Eiger rather than climbed two flights of stairs. She got ready for bed slowly, her movements oddly uncoordinated, then for comfort got out her diary to note the date of her return flight the following month. If Luca went on trying to get his own way, she thought grimly, four whole weeks of holding out against him would take every bit of will-power she possessed.

Georgia sighed, stuck the little pencil back in the slot, then frowned and opened the diary again. Her pupils dilated as she saw an entry in entirely the wrong place. She leafed through a few pages, stared at the entry again, then sagged against the pillows, an arm over her eyes in despair.

CHAPTER ELEVEN

AFTER Marco Sardi returned to his responsibilities at Valorino, Luca Valori was able to spend more time at the Villa Toscana—a circumstance which Georgia reacted to with varying emotions. Far from being daunted by her refusal he seemed spurred on by it, and drove her mad by trying to engineer time alone with her. Marco Sardi was amused. And, Georgia knew, approving. It pleased him to see that the more obvious his charismatic brother-in-law made his pursuit, the farther Georgia retreated.

She kept busy by teaching Alessa, and asked Marco Sardi's permission to drive the child to visit the house where the composer Puccini had lived and some of the other beautiful old houses open to the public in the area. Together she and Alessa looked at fabulous paintings and furniture, and wandered through gardens of breathtaking loveliness, the child happy to do whatever Georgia suggested, even to the point of talking English during the expeditions.

'I don't want to go back to school,' said Alessa mutinously one day.

'Why not?'

'Because when I do you must go away.'

'I'll come and visit you sometimes,' promised Georgia, hoping that she could keep her word. 'Venice isn't very far away. Perhaps your father will bring you to visit me too.'

'Or Luca,' said Alessa eagerly. 'He likes you, Georgia.'

'Like' seemed hardly the word sometimes, thought Georgia drily when she excused herself to go to bed immediately after dinner. As both men rose to their feet the look Luca gave her should have turned her to stone on the spot. His eyes were like discs of blue ice as she said her goodnights and pre-empted any plan that he might have had to speak to her alone.

At the weekends she avoided him by continuing with her exploration of Florence, driving herself there in the Fiat instead of accepting the lift he offered.

Two weeks later, when she returned from a Saturday spent gazing at the paintings in the Pitti Palace, Georgia dined alone with Marco Sardi. Luca, it seemed, had finally given up on her and resumed his normal social life.

'Emilia rang today while you were out,' announced Marco. 'She would be very pleased if you would lunch with her tomorrow, and suggests she send a car for you at noon unless she hears otherwise.'

'How very kind of her,' said Georgia, surprised.

'She knows I am taking Alessa to spend Sunday with my sister and her family, and thought you might like to keep her company.'

Georgia liked the idea a lot, but when Emilia Valori's stately limousine came to collect Georgia the next day the owner was sitting in the back, a rather mischievous smile on her patrician features. The chauffeur jumped out to hand Georgia in beside his mistress, and Emilia patted Georgia's hand.

'I thought it would be more interesting to go out for lunch. Gianni shall drive us through parts of

Tuscany you may not have seen yet, and then we shall stop for a meal at a place I think you will like.'

Georgia shrugged, smiling. 'Whatever you say, *signora*. It's very kind of you to invite me.'

The sharp blue eyes subjected her to a prolonged scrutiny. 'You look tired, my dear. Is Alessa wearing you out?'

'No. It's just the weather. We northerners find it hard to sleep in heat like this.'

Emilia nodded thoughtfully, then turned away to wave a hand at a Palladian mansion perched on a hillside in the distance. She continued to point out various features of her much loved Tuscany as they drove through blinding sunshine which made Georgia glad of the car's efficient air-conditioning.

Eventually Gianni nosed the gleaming black car up a hillside track, negotiated a few hairpin bends with panache and came to a halt in front of a house with slanting, asymmetric roofs and a rustic, arcaded façade which blended well into its setting of hillside vineyards. Rust-red curtains fluttered in the open arches, and a veil of greenery softened the rough creamy stone of the walls.

'Quite an out-of-the-way place for a restaurant,' commented Georgia as she turned to help Emilia Valori out of the car.

'It is not a restaurant, my dear,' confessed the old lady, with no trace of remorse. 'This is La Casupola, the home of my grandson. And here comes Luca himself, to spare me your reproaches.'

Georgia stared, unsmiling, as Luca appeared round the side of the house at a run, dressed in white denims and a blue shirt, his bare feet thrust into faded espadrilles. His hair was wet, and he was buttoning the shirt as he came, and had obviously just taken a bath. He gave both ladies an encompassing smile, kissed his grandmother on both cheeks, then lifted Georgia's rigid hand to his lips.

'Forgive me. I was helping Vito tune the engine of his truck. Welcome to my home, Georgia. And forgive my grandmother also. The deception was mine. You would not have consented to come here any other way, so—' he shrugged '—this was my solution to the problem.'

Georgia gave him a tight, dangerous smile, angry with him because he knew that there was no way she'd make a scene in front of the lady watching the exchange with open enjoyment. 'Why should there be anything to forgive? It's my day off, the sun is shining, and Signora Valori has taken me on a tour of parts of Tuscany I might otherwise never have seen.'

'You are not angry, then,' he commented, standing aside for them to enter.

Georgia avoided an answer by commenting with pleasure on the rustic charm of La Casupola, which, she learned, meant hovel and was Luca's little joke for a home which, if not as sophisticated and luxurious as the Villa Toscana, was much more to her own personal taste.

The house was sparsely furnished with sturdy dark old pieces that Luca had collected together over the years. Old-fashioned mattresses covered in bleached linen cushioned the settles pushed against most of the walls, and hangings everywhere were the rust-red of those which wafted gently in the open arches of the terrace, adding a note of warmth to the stone walls and floors and making a frame for the breathtaking view visible from every window.

Luca installed his grandmother on one of the upright chairs at the table and provided his guests with sparkling white wine, grown, he said, with a look at Georgia, from his own vines. He pulled out a chair for her, then seated himself on the ledge of one of the arches, fit and brown and so good to look at that Georgia felt a pang of something very akin to pain as Luca waved a proprietorial hand at the vista spread out below.

'Do you like my view, Georgia?'

'How could I not?' she said with truth. 'This is the most idyllic bit of Tuscany I've seen so far.'

'You find it quiet after the noisier pleasures of Florence yesterday?' asked Emilia, sipping her wine.

'Peaceful rather than quiet.' Georgia smiled. 'I went to the Pitti Palace to look at all the pictures, and after that I finally managed a visit to David.'

'David?' said the old lady.

'Michelangelo's *David*, Nonna,' said Luca, grinning. 'And were you disappointed?'

Georgia shook her head vigorously. 'No. How could I be? I just stood there for ages in awe. What a masterpiece!'

The meal was brought in by a plump little woman who greeted Emilia Valori with great deference as she brought plates of simple, perfect pasta in a savoury, basil-flavoured tomato sauce.

'Rosa's cooking has not deteriorated, I see,' commented the old lady as she ate sparingly.

'I have not been here very much since Maddalena died,' said Luca, 'but Rosa keeps the place immaculate, and never complains when I arrive unexpectedly. Her husband and son tend the vines,' he added to Georgia, then looked up with a smile as Rosa came in with a streaming tureen, to serve them with dark, strongly flavoured meat in a sauce that Georgia found oddly sweet.

Halfway through the meal she laid down her fork in defeat. 'I shouldn't have eaten so much pasta,' she said apologetically.

'The dish is not to everyone's taste,' agreed Emilia. 'The sauce is made with vinegar, sugar, and chocolate—a local way of preparing hare.'

Hare? Georgia felt her stomach lurch and drank deeply of her glass of mineral water, averting her eyes from her plate.

'Forgive me—I asked Rosa to make a true Tuscan speciality. You would like something else?' said Luca quickly, and she shook her head.

'No, thank you. Just some water, please.'

When the meal was over Emilia Valori announced her intention of a nap on one of the padded settles. Luca piled cushions behind her, kissed her cheek, then looked at Georgia in enquiry.

'Would you like to rest too? Or would you prefer a tour of my home, then a walk outside once the sun is less fierce?'

Georgia nodded, still troubled by memories of the Tuscan way with hare, and followed him up wide stone stairs to the upper floor, where the same russet curtains hung at windows in rooms painted to harmonise with the stone of the house. A pair of vibrant oils of local scenery lit up a wall of a room which was obviously Luca's inner sanctum. Books were piled on tables beside deep leather chairs and couches, and as well as the expected television and video recorder there was a stereo, a fax machine and a computer.

'So you can keep in touch with the outside world even as you relax,' commented Georgia. In deference to what she'd believed was a visit to Emilia Valori she wore a dark blue dress of cotton voile dotted in white. The filmy material floated slightly in the breeze from the open windows as she examined compact discs on a shelf near the stereo system, her profile turned to the man who stood leaning against a wall, arms folded, his eyes on her face.

'Why are you so remote?' he asked abruptly, in a voice so harsh and yet so musical that Georgia had to steel herself against its appeal. 'I thought we agreed to be friends,' he added, moving from the wall. 'But you are no longer friendly, Georgia, and there is so little time before you go away.'

She turned very deliberately and met the brilliant blue gaze with eyes as black and expressionless as jet. 'I'll be honest, Luca. You are a very attractive man. In many more ways than looks,' she added, and held up a hand as he started towards her. 'No. Please don't touch me, because we both know what will happen if you do. And I can't let it happen, for reasons we've already discussed. So, for the time left to me at the Villa Toscana, will you leave me alone, please?'

'I cannot leave you alone! I never thought to say the words to any woman in my life, but it is no use. I am in love with you!' he said rapidly, swallowing hard as though the words had choked him. 'How can you look at me so coldly, like a woman made of marble?'

Since Georgia felt very hot, and beads of perspiration were standing out on her upper lip, this was a very strange question, she thought in a detached, dazed kind of way. She moved towards him in sudden appeal. 'Luca—bathroom—please?' she said in hoarse, peremptory English.

Her urgency galvanised him into action, and seconds later Georgia was alone in a cool, white-tiled bathroom, parting with the hare and the pasta and what seemed like everything she'd eaten for several days. Afterwards she staggered outside to find Luca waiting for her on the landing.

'Georgia—you look like a ghost!' he exclaimed, keeping to English. 'Come, *cara*, lie down on my bed for a while.'

'But your grandmother—' she protested feebly.

Luca swept her objections aside. 'She will understand. And I shall leave you alone,' he added bitterly. 'You need fear no further assault on your virtue, I swear.'

Georgia's virtue—old-fashioned word, she thought muzzily—was her last concern at the moment. She let Luca lead her to a large, cool room with curtains drawn against the afternoon sunlight. He sat her gently on a wide bed with a carved wood headboard, then disappeared through a door. She heard water running and then felt a cool, damp cloth on her forehead as he bathed away the perspiration.

'Rest now,' he said as he laid her against the pillows. 'I shall return later. Sleep, *carissima*.'

Georgia obeyed gratefully, and woke later from a deep, dreamless sleep to find Luca standing at the edge of the bed. She sat up with a jerk, then moaned, putting a hand to her head as it reeled, and Luca leapt to lay her back against the pillows, his face strangely stern.

'Signora Valori—' began Georgia, but Luca laid a finger on her lips.

'She begs your forgiveness, but was obliged to return home for an appointment with a friend for dinner—'

'But I should have gone with her—'

'No.' Luca stood looking down at her in a way which did very little to improve Georgia's well-being. 'We must talk, you and I. And talk here, away from Marco and Alessa and all interruption, until certain matters are cleared between us.'

'I can't see why,' she returned, shivering a little despite the heat.

'You soon will. When you are ready, come downstairs and Rosa will bring tea. I have brought your handbag. It is here alongside the bed.'

As the door closed behind him Georgia sat up experimentally. This time the room stayed still; she got to her feet carefully, and found her legs steady enough to carry her to Luca's austere, functional bathroom. Nothing of the sybarite here, she thought as she dashed her face with cold water. A few minutes later, feeling better, she touched her mouth with lipstick, brushed her hair and went from the room to descend the shallow stone stairs to the ground floor. Luca rose from the table as she reached the terrace.

'Sit down, please, Georgia,' he said, pulling out a chair.

She obeyed, eyeing him warily. This was a very different Luca from the passionate, persuasive man of only an hour or so before. Well, two hours, she amended, after a glance at her watch. Her sleep had been longer than she'd thought. She was about to ask what was wrong when a concerned, anxious Rosa brought a tea-tray and begged the *signorina* to say if there was anything she wished to accompany the tea.

'No, nothing, thank you,' replied Georgia, with a grateful smile. 'Just tea will be wonderful.'

There was an awkward silence after Rosa had gone. Georgia asked if Luca would like tea, but he shook his head, and she sipped thirstily, wishing miserably that Signora Valori could have waited for her.

'I had a talk with my grandmother while you were sleeping,' said Luca at last. 'It was very instructive. It showed me what a stupid fool I've been.'

Georgia frowned. 'A fool?'

He nodded, his face sombre. 'First because, as Nonna said, only a fool would have tried to seduce someone we, as a family, were responsible for.'

It was fortunate for Georgia that for once he was speaking slowly and deliberately, instead of the usual liquid, rapid Italian that sometimes left her grasping for nuances of meaning. She poured herself another cup of tea, and drank a little of it as Luca went on speaking.

'I had no excuse for what I did,' he said tonelessly. 'I knew about this James of yours, also your sister's husband. But it was this very knowledge which drove me to show you that as a lover I could make you forget both of them. I was so sure that once you were in my arms you would discover this, but when we were together at last, alone, your body against mine—' His mouth twisted. 'For the first time in my life I lost control, I ignored your protests, blind to everything other than my desire for you.'

Georgia eyed him uneasily, experiencing a sinking feeling nothing to do with the hare.

Suddenly his head lifted and the blue, searching eyes held hers relentlessly. 'My grandmother pointed out to me this afternoon that you could be expecting my child.'

Since, for the past two weeks, Georgia had been tortured by the same suspicions, she found nothing to say, and the colour drained from Luca's face.

'You *are* pregnant?' he demanded hoarsely, and she shrugged miserably.

'I don't know—'

'But nature is giving you warning that you might be,' he said with tact.

She breathed in deeply. 'I'm afraid so. It's never happened—or *not* happened before, so I suppose it's possible I may be. It seems so *unfair*,' she added with sudden passion.

Luca winced, and passed a hand over his face. He took a handkerchief from his pocket and mopped his brow, looking as sick as Georgia had felt earlier. 'I will arrange a visit to Dr Fassi. It is important that we know as soon as possible.'

'Why?' she said stonily.

He glared at her, outraged. 'Why? Surely that is obvious!'

'If I'm pregnant,' she said in English, just to make sure she made it clear, 'I shall deal with the problem myself. I want nothing from you.'

Luca sprang up, pulling her from her chair. 'What is this "deal with the problem"?' he demanded. '*Un aborto*? Is this what you intend?'

Whereupon Georgia slapped his incensed face as hard as she could and bent to pick up her bag. 'Drive me back to the villa, please,' she ordered, her voice shaking with fury.

'Not until you tell me what you mean to do,' he said roughly, catching both her hands in his.

'All right,' she said through her teeth. 'I intend to go back to England in two weeks, after which I hope never to see you again in my life.'

'Then your hopes will not be realised,' he spat back. 'If you are carrying my child I will marry you.'

'I don't *want* you to marry me!'

He shrugged indifferently. 'So? You will marry me nevertheless. A Valori honours his debts. I am to blame for your—your condition. Therefore I will make reparation.'

'But you can't!' she said breathlessly. 'If we marry we're stuck with each other for life. It's the reason I've never got involved before. I'm a Catholic, just like you.'

'Ah, I see,' he said, enlightened. 'This is why you struck me when I mentioned abortion.'

'No, it's *not*,' she flung at him, even more enraged. 'It wouldn't matter if I was a Hindu or a Seventh-day Adventist or any other religion you care to name. I resented your assumption. Anyway, the solution to my little problem—'

'*Our* problem,' he corrected.

Georgia pulled her hands from his. 'No, Luca,' she said wearily. 'The problem's mine. I have no intention of marrying you. A single parent is no novelty in England. I'll cope with *my* problem the way I think fit. And it certainly doesn't include marrying someone who doesn't want to marry anyone at all, let alone me.'

Luca thrust a hand through his hair, scowling blackly at her. 'That was before I knew—'

'We don't know yet,' she interrupted, though deep down inside she did. Somehow.

'Then why were you so ill this afternoon?'

'It was the hare.'

'I don't think so.'

'Think what you like,' she snapped. 'Now please take me back to the villa. And don't you dare breathe a word of this to Signor Sardi.'

'You think I wish to broadcast my stupidity?' he demanded, and stalked ahead of her to where the Supremo lay waiting beside the house.

Georgia eyed the car reluctantly, pushing the heavy hair back from her face. 'For once,' she said wearily in English, 'will you drive slowly, please? I still feel a bit fragile.'

Luca stared at her in resentment for a moment, then his face changed dramatically and he took her in his arms, holding her gingerly as though she were an invalid. 'Forgive me, Georgia—I have no right to be angry. The blame is mine. I shall make sure everyone knows that.'

Georgia leaned against him for a moment, then stepped back, squaring her shoulders. 'No need for that,' she said briskly. 'Once I'm back in England no one here need know a thing about it.'

'*I* know,' he threw back at her, opening the car door. 'So does my grandmother—and Elsa. It is a secret no longer. One more, in the person of Dr Fassi, can hardly make any difference.'

'I have no intention of seeing Dr Fassi,' retorted Georgia, and closed her eyes quickly as Luca began the tortuous descent to the road.

Her protests were in vain. Next morning Dr Fassi came to see her before lessons began, after Marco Sardi and Luca had left for Valorino.

'Luca says you were ill yesterday at the farm,' he said, smiling at her scarlet face. 'So Elsa will come with us to your room. I shall take a look at you to make sure all is well.'

A day or two later Dr Fassi called again, took Georgia aside and told her that the tests he'd done were positive.

'Don't look so tragic, my dear,' he said gently. 'Luca says you will be married as soon as possible.'

'You've already told *Luca*?' said Georgia, shattered.

'He instructed me to do so.'

It was pointless to lose her temper with Dr Fassi, Georgia reminded herself, and managed a smile as he took his farewell.

She moved through the day with the smile pinned to her dazed face, in an attempt to allay Alessa's anxiety. The little girl was very worried by two visits from Dr Fassi, and had to be reassured by mention of a stomach bug which was now better.

'I am glad to see you recovered,' said Marco Sardi at dinner that night, which to Georgia's mingled dismay and relief they ate alone. Luca was away for a few days on a business trip again, she was told, and gave herself a scathing lecture because she felt abandoned. After dinner that evening Georgia was called to the telephone to speak to Signora Valori.

'You will forgive an old woman for her interference,' was the lady's opening gambit. 'It was necessary for Luca to know the damage he had done.'

'How did you know there was any damage?' asked Georgia faintly.

'Call it womanly intuition, or anxiety, or anything you like, but the moment I saw you on Sunday I was convinced I was right. Your reaction to the hare only confirmed my suspicions. I thought Luca should share them. He tells me I am right.'

'Yes,' said Georgia miserably.

'Do not upset yourself, my child. Luca will marry you as soon as you wish.'

'But I don't want him to. It isn't necessary these days. Times have changed. I don't want a husband.'

'They are very useful in certain circumstances,' said Emilia Valori drily. 'And in this one I think you will find you have no choice.'

She was right. When Luca returned to the villa two evenings later he sent Pina up to Georgia's room to demand her presence in the garden before dinner. She went down a few minutes later to find him by the pool, staring into the water. When her reflection appeared beside his he turned sharply.

'How are you?' he demanded, taking her hands in his.

Georgia tugged them away, her face stony. 'You know how I am.'

'I have just returned from a visit to your parents,' he said abruptly, taking her breath away. 'I have told them exactly what happened.'

'You did *what*?' Georgia stared at him, appalled. 'You had no business to talk to them before I did. How dare you?'

He ignored her, speaking rapidly—so rapidly that it was difficult for her to follow him. 'I confessed all, then I asked for your hand in marriage, and after a while, when your charming parents had recovered from so great a shock, they agreed that this was the only solution possible—for both of us.'

'And if I don't fall in with all this?' she said wrathfully.

'But you will,' he said with sudden authority. 'It is not what either of us would have wished. I admit it freely. But, since you are to bear my child, you have no choice. You will marry me, Georgia, as soon as it can be arranged. Afterwards the way you choose to conduct our marriage will be up to you. The child, of course, will be my concern.'

'It will not! I may be pregnant by accident, but one thing you can be very sure of, Luca Valori—my child will be *my* concern.' She glanced up at him, her eyes flashing in the sunset light, and Luca shrugged.

'Then you have no choice. My son—or my daughter—must be born here in Tuscany, to grow up here as a Valori.'

'You mean that if I refuse to be parted from my child I must do the same,' she said wearily.

'Is it so great a sacrifice?' he said softly, taking her hand. 'We agreed to be friends, remember. We can be husband and wife and still remain friends, Georgia.'

'Have you any idea,' she began slowly, choosing the words with care, 'what it will be like for me, knowing you are chained to me in a marriage you don't want?'

Luca's face set, adding years suddenly to his finely chiselled good looks. 'I was blind to all except my own desires that afternoon. I took what you were not willing to give, and the gods have a saying, do they not? Take what you want, and then pay for it.'

CHAPTER TWELVE

STARS hung like diamonds in a black velvet sky as Luca turned the Supremo up the private road to La Casupola on the evening of Georgia's wedding day. Lights were burning in all the windows as Rosa and her husband, Vito, came out to welcome their young master home with his bride.

Luca, to the delight of everyone except his wife, picked Georgia up and carried her over the threshold, then set her down and turned to shake Vito's hand and receive a kiss from Rosa, a look from her bridegroom prompting Georgia to do the same.

When Rosa was sure that Georgia lacked nothing for her comfort, and Vito had taken the luggage upstairs, the couple left to retire to their own home in the village a mile away and the newly-weds were left alone.

Georgia stood in the middle of the room feeling lonely and alien. The light from two rose-shaded bronze lamps flanking the stone fireplace merely seemed to emphasise the dark shadows beyond their radius.

'Rosa has left us a cold supper,' said Luca quietly. 'Would you like a rest before eating, or a bath?'

Georgia nodded silently, and he waved her before him up the wide, shallow stairs. She hesitated on the threshold of Luca's bedroom. Nothing had been discussed about sleeping arrangements. Vito, naturally, had placed all the luggage in the master bedroom.

Luca took her by the hand and led her inside. 'The bed is large. And we shall both share it. I shall not touch you.'

'Surely there's another bedroom,' said Georgia coldly.

'There are two.'

'Then I shall sleep in one of them.'

Luca barred her way to the door. 'No, you will not. You are my bride. And Rosa looks after this house. I do not wish it known that you refuse to sleep with me. But sleep,' he added grimly, 'is the only thing required of you. I forced you once. I shall not do so again.' He took off his tie and threw his jacket on a chair on his way to the door. 'Please come downstairs when you are ready to eat.'

Georgia watched him go, feeling strangely detached, as though the events of the day had happened to someone else. A brief ceremony in London early that morning had joined her in marriage to Gianluca Valori, since nothing he or her parents could say would persuade her to the full church ceremony with nuptial mass. It had been strange to stand before the priest with only Marco Sardi and an ecstatic Alessa to witness it, alone with her parents and Tom and Charlotte, all of whom, she knew very well, were still reeling secretly from the surprise of it all.

John Fleming had insisted on paying for a wedding breakfast at the Ritz, to gild his younger daughter's wedding day with at least a little glamour, and surprisingly enough it had been a very festive meal. For her parents' sake Georgia did her best to smile and join in, purely to reassure her family that she was happy with the future that Luca had mapped out for her so relentlessly.

Though, to be fair, she thought as she undressed, the bride-to-be had taken so little interest in the wedding that in the end Luca had lost patience, his only consultations made with her mother and father, who were rather happier about the whole thing than she was. Her parents had always been rather lukewarm about her relationship with James Astin, and made no secret of being very much taken with Luca. They made it plain to their daughter that they admired his impeccable reaction to the situation. Even Charlotte and Tom had obviously liked him more than anticipated.

Luca had been stiffly courteous at first, but, after the relaxing effect of the vintage champagne they were served, unbent to Tom, who took Luca's initial reserve as awkwardness with the situation rather than anything personal. Alessa, of course, was a big hit with everyone. Anne Fleming was entranced with the child's careful English, and deeply touched by Alessa's joy at having Georgia for her very own aunt now that she was married to Luca.

'And when I live in England, will you visit us?' asked Alessa eagerly, and was assured that all Georgia's family would be only too delighted to visit the Sardi home and welcomed both Alessa and her father to theirs whenever they wished.

In fact, thought Georgia, yawning, everybody loved everybody except the bride and groom, who had barely exchanged two words on the flight to Pisa, and very few more on the drive from the airport to La Casupola. The time before the wedding had been a dream-like, unreal period to Georgia, who had hoped against hope, right up to the last minute, that somehow a miracle would happen to prevent it. But nothing had, and here she was, Signora Valori no less, with a few ordeals stretching in front of her as Luca planned to take her to meet not only his relations but Marco Sardi's as well.

She had flatly refused a conventional honeymoon, and the only concession made to it was Luca's absence from Valorino for the first two weeks of his marriage. To display to the world at large, he'd said to Georgia, in one of their rare moments of privacy before she flew back to England to prepare for the wedding, that their marriage was as normal as possible. She could call it face-saving on his part, hypocrisy, or anything else she liked, but a honeymoon of sorts she would have, whether she wanted it or not.

The other reason for Georgia's feeling of unreality was her health. The hare, it seemed, had been the real culprit for her stomach upset after all on her last visit to La Casupola. The baby was causing her no problems at all, either with her digestion or her shape. If anything, she was thinner in places than usual, which she wouldn't have noticed if her mother hadn't commented on it when the oyster silk suit bought for the wedding had been a little on the loose side when the time came to wear it.

Secretly Georgia had hoped that Dr Fassi's tests were wrong, and once back in England bought herself a pregnancy testing kit and did her own tests. But there was no mistake. One brief sexual encounter with Luca Valori had been all it took to turn her entire life upside down.

Once out of the bath Georgia brushed out her hair, which had been twisted up in a sophisticated coiffeur to complement the wickedly expensive hat that her mother had insisted she buy.

'Either that or you wear some flowers in your hair,'
Anne Fleming had said, and Georgia, rejecting anything as bridal as flowers, had worn a straw tricorne
tilted low on her forehead, with a wide-meshed veil
to hide the reluctance in her eyes during the brief
ceremony. But in the end her refusal of flowers had
been useless after all. When she arrived at the church
a radiant, excited Alessa had been waiting with two
posies of creamy rosebuds—a small one for herself
and a larger one for the bride. And during the
ceremony Luca had slid a circlet of gold encrusted
with rubies on her finger instead of the expected plain
gold band, and afterwards kissed her squarely on the
mouth before yielding her to the usual barrage of
kissing from the rest of the party.

Georgia swathed herself in a bathtowel and went
out into the bedroom to search in a suitcase for something to wear, hesitated, then with a wry little smile
took out the amber satin nightgown and peignoir that
Charlotte had bought her.

'I'd look terrible in that colour, but with your hair
and eyes you'll look good enough to eat,' had been
her sister's verdict, and Georgia slid the nightgown
over her head, then examined herself in the long
cheval-glass which she rather thought was new since
her last visit to Luca's bedroom. The nightgown was
in her usual size, but showed rather more of her breasts
than she would have liked. She leaned forward in surprise as she saw that they were visibly fuller. She might
be thinner as yet in her lower half, but the rest of her
was definitely burgeoning.

Georgia wrapped herself hurriedly in the peignoir,
tied the sash tightly, slid her feet into satin mules rather
more glamorous than her usual scruffy espadrilles

and, with a last, doubtful look in the mirror, left the room and went noiselessly downstairs. The stairs led directly into the living room, and halfway down she paused to look at Luca, who was sitting on one of the padded settles, his legs stretched out in front of him and a glass of what looked like whisky in one hand as he stared into space with an air of depression that no self-respecting bridegroom should have worn. She sighed and his head went up, his eyes meeting hers as she went slowly down the last few steps to the room.

'I wasn't sure if you were here or in your room upstairs,' she said awkwardly as he rose to his feet, her face hot at the look his lids fell like shutters to hide.

'After we have eaten we can drink coffee there—or some of your famous tea, if you prefer,' said Luca. 'How do you feel?'

'A little tired from the travelling. Otherwise very well.'

'*Bene.*' He smiled. 'Have you noticed how good I am?'

'Good?' She smiled back involuntarily.

'I have spoken only English all day,' he pointed out.

Georgia chuckled. 'So you have.'

'Just for this day, you understand, in deference to my English bride.' Luca waved a hand towards the trio of shallow steps that led to the dining room. 'Come. Our wedding breakfast was a long time ago.'

'You should have eaten something on the plane,' said Georgia as he held the door open for her; then she exclaimed in delight at the lighted candles and the posy of flowers that Rosa had arranged with such loving care. 'How lovely!'

Luca pulled out a chair and bowed ceremoniously. 'Sit. For tonight only I will wait on you.'

Feeling a great deal better in more ways than her physical health, Georgia watched in pretended amazement as Luca fetched a series of dishes from the refrigerator in the kitchen, laughing as he served her with mock formality and with his own hands dressed her salad with the celebrated local olive oil.

'Rosa wished to serve us,' said Luca as he attacked his meal with appetite. 'But she understood when I told her I wanted to be alone with my bride.'

'Why did you?' said Georgia bluntly, buttering a thick slice of *ciabatta* bread.

'I thought my bride would prefer it.' Luca gave her a brilliant blue look. 'This way no pretence is necessary, and we can dine like the friends we have agreed to be. Let us toast the agreement in this excellent Brunello.'

'You speak very good English,' she commented. 'I don't know why you make me speak Italian all the time.'

He laughed and filled her glass with ruby-coloured wine. 'Because your accent charms me, and the mistakes you make are very—' he frowned in thought '—*accattivante*?'

'Endearing,' said Georgia, flushing again.

Luca smiled. 'I hope you feel the same about my mistakes, *tesoro*.' His face darkened abruptly. 'Except for one, of course. That I think you will never forgive.'

Georgia laid down her knife and fork. 'Luca, let's put our cards on the table—be very honest with each other,' she added as he raised an enquiring eyebrow. 'I know it sounds odd, but right up to the moment we were married I hoped, by some miracle, it wouldn't be necessary—'

'You hoped to lose the baby?' he shot at her, eyes glittering.

'No!' She stared at him, startled. 'No. I didn't want that.'

'Then what miracle were you hoping for?' he demanded. 'That I would change my mind about wanting to bring up my own child?'

Georgia's shoulders sagged. 'Put like that, it does sound rather silly. Anyway, what I'm trying to say is, now that we *are* married I'll try to make the best of it.'

'*Va bene*—so shall I.' He reached out a long, slim hand and Georgia put hers into it, giving him a smile which turned into a yawn.

'Sorry, Luca. I think the day finally caught up with me.'

'*Allora*—come to bed. Leave all these things to Rosa in the morning.' He stood up, holding her eyes with his. 'I made no mistake of English tenses when I said, Come. If I leave you to go to bed alone you will lie wakeful and tense waiting for me to join you. So we shall prepare for the night together, and talk like the friends we have decided to be, and you will not feel awkward and nervous. You have nothing to fear from me, Georgia.'

'I know.' She gave him a rather shy smile. 'You'll have to make allowances. I've never shared a room with a man before.'

He grinned in response. 'Neither have I!'

Georgia woke in the night to a feeling of strangeness which she realised came not only from her surroundings but from the fact that she was sharing a bed with someone who took up a great deal of room. Luca Valori, accustomed to sleeping alone in his huge bed, was lying diagonally across it.

She lay curled up, quiet as a mouse, afraid to disturb him by trying to shove him over. They had survived the slight awkwardness of getting ready for bed very well, and for a while had lain talking over their wedding day before, to her intense astonishment, Georgia realised that she couldn't keep awake. She smiled in the darkness. If someone had told her this morning that she'd share a bed with her elegant, rather remote bridegroom and fall asleep very happily in the process, she would have laughed them to scorn. But Luca was right. It was better to start as they meant to go on. Or as Luca meant them to go on.

'You are awake,' said a deep, husky voice in the darkness, and the long legs retreated, giving her more room. 'Forgive me, Georgia, I have almost pushed you out of bed.'

She chuckled. 'I didn't like to push you back—'

'In case you woke me,' he interrupted, resigned. 'I gave you my word, Georgia. You can sleep in peace.'

Which had rather too much of a churchyard flavour, she thought, pulling a face. 'I know that. I was just being polite.'

Luca gave a smothered chuckle, and turned on the lamp beside his bed. He raised himself on an elbow to look at her. 'I am thirsty. Would you like something?'

Georgia nodded. 'Fruit juice?'

'Whatever you want.' He stood up, gave a stretch which threatened the silk pyjama trousers tied round his narrow hips, wrapped himself in a dark robe and went from the room.

While he was away Georgia paid a visit to the bathroom, brushed her hair, laughed at herself for doing so, and was back in the wide, carved bed, propped up against the pillows, when Luca returned with wine, fruit juice and glasses on a tray which he put down on the table beside him.

'Would you care for some champagne in your orange juice?' he said, shrugging off his robe. 'I think it can do little harm.'

'At three in the morning?' said Georgia, laughing to hide a frisson of response to the muscular beauty of his torso. 'A bit decadent.'

Lifting a negligent shoulder, Luca handed her a glass, filled one for himself, then slid in beside her and leaned back, relaxed, against the pale, carved wood of the bedhead. 'But tonight is a special occasion, Georgia.' He glanced sideways at her, his eyes softening. 'Is it so very difficult for you, *innamorata*, to think of yourself as my wife?'

When he called her 'sweetheart' it was remarkably easy. Georgia gave him a look from beneath her lashes. 'No. Now that it's signed and sealed it's easier to cope with, somehow.'

'Then you do not hate me any more?'

'I've never hated you, Luca!'

'But you would not allow yourself to fall in love with me.' He stared down into his glass. 'I wish that I had such iron British control over my own emotions,' he added suddenly in his own swift, melodic tongue. 'I need to confess, Georgia.'

'Confess?' she asked, wondering if she understood him properly.

'When I said you must sleep here with me it was nothing to do with Rosa, or anyone other than myself. I had a feeling here—' he struck himself in the chest '—that if we began to sleep apart from the first night our marriage would have no hope of success.' He turned his head and looked down into her intent eyes. 'Also I am human. You are beautiful and my wife, and I wanted to share a bed with you.'

Georgia drained her glass and held it out for more, smiling mischievously. 'I know you did.'

Luca leaned over to fill her glass and handed it back to her. 'You made no protest,' he said, in a tone which made her pulse quicken.

'No. It—it seemed only fair.' She drank from the glass, then looked up at him accusingly. 'You forgot the orange juice!'

'No. I did not forget. I am trying to seduce you with champagne—and patience,' he said candidly, his smile doing so much for his cause that Georgia, conscious of a glow that had nothing to do with the wine, smiled back, shaking her head.

'You said I could conduct our marriage any way I liked,' she reminded him.

'Have I tried to impose my will?' he returned, his eyes glittering under lowered lids.

'I rather think that's what you're doing right now!' Georgia finished the wine and handed him the glass.

Luca set both their glasses on the tray, then turned casually and drew her into his arms so that she lay against his chest with her face turned up to his. 'This friendship of ours should allow a little contact, Georgia.'

Relaxed by the exquisite wine, comfortable in the embrace of arms which held her loosely rather than constricting her, she nodded casually. 'Yes.'

'Good. Because now we are married there is one question I must ask.'

She frowned, tilting her head back to see his face more clearly. 'What is it?'

'Today I met Tom Hannay, and liked him more than I believed possible,' said Luca gruffly. 'But that night—'

'Which night?'

'At the Lucchesi in Florence. My room was on the same floor as yours, Georgia. I had asked after you at Reception because I wished to speak with you on the phone, to introduce myself and make arrangements for the next day.'

She stirred restlessly, but his arms tightened.

'Let me finish.' He breathed in deeply. 'As I went up to dress for dinner that evening I saw Tom Hannay come out of your room, obviously naked under his bathrobe.'

'So *that's* why you thought he was my lover!' Georgia shook with laughter against his bare chest. 'You thought he was sneaking back to his wife after a session in my bed?'

'You may think it funny, but I did not,' he said rapidly, holding her tightly. 'I had already seen you on the plane. I thought fortune was smiling on me when I discovered that my beautiful fellow passenger was the teacher Marco had engaged for Alessa. Then I saw Tom leave your room and—'

'Thought the worst,' she said, resigned. 'I wasn't even *in* the room, Luca. Charlotte was sick when we got to the hotel. I stayed with her while Tom had a shower in my bathroom. Charlotte asked him to in case she needed theirs in a hurry again.'

Luca stared down into her eyes in astonishment. 'You mean I have tortured myself all these weeks for nothing?' His eyes narrowed suddenly. 'But there is still this James of yours.' He shook her gently. 'I hoped you would invite him to the wedding so that he could watch as we became man and wife.'

'Oh, did you? James would have hated it.' Georgia sighed. 'I feel guilty because I rather made use of James, used him as a sort of barrier to try to keep you at a distance.' She sighed ruefully. 'Before I met you I'd found your countrymen appreciative but very respectful. You—well, you were different.'

'I was different because I fell in love with you,' he said with heat. 'You know very well that I wanted you from the first. And when you had the accident I was out of my mind for a while, enough to believe that if I made love to you I would erase these lovers of yours from your mind and you would fall in love with me. But my plan failed.'

'Not really,' muttered Georgia against his chest, and felt him tense.

He held her away from him. 'Say what you mean!' he commanded.

'I was already in love with you anyway,' she said unevenly. 'I tried so hard not to be, Luca, but it was no use. I wasn't *forced* to marry you. This isn't the Middle Ages. If I'd really wanted to bring up my child alone nothing could have stopped me. I married you because, deep down, I wanted to.'

'You love me?' he demanded imperiously.

'I suppose I must do.'

He let out an explosive sigh and bent his head to hers in a kiss which went on so long that both were breathless and shaking when he raised his head.

'*Carissima*,' he breathed, and with unsteady hands began to caress the full, ripe curves only partially veiled in amber silk. Suddenly he closed his eyes in anguish and pulled away.

'*Dio*—I forgot!'

'Forgot what?' she said crossly.

'The child—'

'He won't mind.'

'Are you sure?' Luca held her close, rubbing his cheek against her hair. 'I am on fire for you, Georgia. You can feel that I am.'

Her cheeks flamed as he splayed a long-fingered hand at the base of her spine to pull her hard against him. 'It *is* our wedding night,' she said breathlessly, and tilted her head back to look into his eyes, her own so brilliant with promise that Luca let out a great, unsteady sigh, and slowly, delicately, taking undisguised pleasure in the task, took off the nightgown and laid her flat on the bed, his eyes moving over her in a caress so arousing that she stirred restlessly and held up her arms to him in an invitation he accepted with triumph.

He smiled into her glittering, heavy eyes and began, with patience, and all the skill and subtlety at his command, to erase all memory of their previous encounter. He made love to her with such self-control that she was helpless and pleading before he surrendered to his own need and took her to dizzying heights of pleasure, all the while telling her how beautiful, how exquisite she was and how much he loved her, the liquid Italian love words interspersed with English so that the brand new Signora Valori was left in no possible doubt about how much she meant to the man she'd married only hours before.

Afterwards they lay entwined in the warm darkness as their heartbeats slowed, and Luca laid a hand on her stomach, his fingers caressing.

'It is hard to believe,' he whispered.

Georgia stretched luxuriously, putting her hand on his to keep it in place. 'I know. Charlotte's sick all the time, but so far I just get a bit sleepy in the evenings.'

'A very desirable habit for a bride,' chuckled Luca against her throat.

Georgia reached up to smooth his untidy hair. 'I wasn't being awkward about a honeymoon, darling. I really did want to start our marriage here, in your home.'

'Our home,' he contradicted, kissing her. 'And I am glad. Here at La Casupola we are not required to do anything. We can stay exactly where we are as long as we want. But there is a pool behind the house if you wish to swim, and we can go to Lucca or Florence to dine whenever you like.'

'You may be glad to in a day or two,' said Georgia, hoping she wasn't right. 'I might bore you.'

Luca rolled over to capture her beneath him, easing his weight on one hip with such practised expertise that Georgia noted it wryly. 'You will never bore me.'

'If I do I can always get a job, go back to the school and teach,' she teased.

'You can if you wish,' he said, surprising her, then spoilt the effect by caressing her in a way which sent everything out of her head but her body's responses to his touch. 'But I hope very much you will not, *innamorata*. I must find a way to persuade you to spend your time here. With me.'

Dawn was lighting up the Tuscan hills before they slept, and it was some time later in the morning, when they were sharing the breakfast brought to the terrace by a beaming Rosa, before Luca raised a quizzical eyebrow at his wife.

'So, Georgia. This marriage of ours. It is better than you expected?'

She put down her cup of coffee and gave the matter due consideration. 'If you mean the bed part, yes. Thank you for your patience in making it so beautiful for me.'

'I wished to atone for the other time,' he said soberly. 'Also I was afraid at first to harm you in any way.'

Georgia smiled mischievously. 'You forgot about that after a while.'

'I know.' The sombre look remained. 'Georgia, I want a promise from you.'

'I made a few in church yesterday,' she pointed out.

'I want you to promise to tell me if you feel in the least ill at any time—until the baby arrives,' he added, his eyes shadowed.

Georgia's face softened. 'Ah, I see. Of course I promise. Though I feel on top of the world right now.' She thought for a moment, trying to think of some way to reassure him, then her eyes lit with inspiration. 'Luca, do you think I look like my mother?'

He looked surprised. 'Why, yes, I do. Your mother is a beautiful woman.'

'And strong as a horse.' Georgia shot a look at him. 'You know that my father's the Catholic? Mother isn't anything in particular.'

'You are trying to tell me something, *carissima*?' he asked, frowning.

'There are precisely eleven months between Charlotte and me, and Charlotte was born exactly nine months from my parents' wedding day. Both of us took only a few hours to arrive, with no complications. But after that Mother decided to take matters into her own hands to avoid having a baby every year. Otherwise,' added Georgia, with a grin, 'heaven knows how many sisters and brothers I might have had. But the point is that, just like Mother, I'm not sick in the mornings, I feel even better than usual, and my only problem lately has been the feeling that you were trapped into a marriage you would never have dreamed of making otherwise.'

'Whereas to have you belong to me is a dream come true,' stated Luca with emphasis. 'The mere thought of losing you changed my mind about marriage.'

Georgia gave him such an incandescent smile that he leapt to his feet and took her in his arms, kissing her with a fervour she responded to in kind.

'So no more worrying,' she said when she could speak.

'I will try,' he promised.

She smiled up at him. 'Luca, I know it's our honeymoon, but could we go and see your grandmother today, since she didn't feel up to coming to the wedding? I want to tell her how much I like being another Signora Valori. And how grateful I am for what she insists on calling her "interference"!'

* * *

On a bright, windy Palm Sunday the following year Georgia and Gianluca Valori joined with the crowds in the black and white marble beauty of the Duomo in Siena to hear mass, their blue-eyed son gazing up at the bright lights and crowing at the music from the safety of his father's arms.

As they moved slowly to the door afterwards, through the tourists massed at the back to watch the service, Luca obtained three palms in the shape of olive branches, one of which he presented to his wife, who thanked him with a kiss. He put one into the tiny, clutching fist of his son, then tucked the third into his jacket pocket, and smiled at Georgia as they emerged into bright, dazzling sunshine.

'I've got one too,' said Alessa, who was following behind with her father and great-grandmother. She hurried to gaze adoringly at the baby. 'He was so good, Georgia; he didn't cry.'

'No,' said Georgia, chuckling. 'He's fine out in company. He prefers to demand attention at night.'

'He is male,' muttered Luca in an undertone, enjoying the colour which rose in his wife's cheeks as she met the look in his eyes.

'This was a very charming idea of yours, Luca,' said Emilia Valori, joining in with her own share of baby-worship. 'Thank you for bringing me here today.'

'I wished to give thanks for the safe arrival of my son, and the well-being of my wife,' he said simply, 'and Georgia is very drawn to Siena, so here we are.'

'You look very well, Georgia,' commented Marco Sardi as they walked towards the great, fan-shaped square.

'I feel well. I did all along.' Georgia gave her husband a grin. 'It was Luca who suffered, not me.'

'She assured me that in her family such things happen with the minimum of fuss,' agreed Luca, surrendering the baby to Georgia. He pulled a face. 'Nevertheless, I was glad when it was all over.'

'So, no doubt, was Georgia.' said his grandmother drily. 'And how is Charlotte's little one?'

'She's so cute,' said Alessa, who had become a regular visitor to the Hannay household since her move to London, a factor which had done much to reconcile her to her temporary stay in England. 'Her name is Flora, Bisnonna. But little Carlo is more beautiful, I think.'

'Since he has his mother's hair and his father's eyes he can hardly fail to be,' said Emilia Valori with satisfaction.

The family party enjoyed lunch together then separated afterwards to go their different ways—Signora Valori to her home in Lucca, Alessa and Marco to the Villa Toscana—while Luca drove his wife and son home to Rosa, who suffered withdrawal symptoms if the baby was out of her sight for long.

When the baby had been fed and changed and put down for a nap Georgia sat with Luca in his *studio* upstairs, so that they could hear if Carlo cried. Luca drew his wife down beside him on one of the sofas, and held her close in his arms as he rubbed his cheek against the thick, coiled hair, then began pulling the pins from it so that it fell to her shoulders in the way he liked best.

'You look too cool, too perfect with your hair up,' he said, and ran his hands through the heavy strands before kissing Georgia's willing mouth. He smiled as he raised his head.

'What is it?' she whispered, curling against him.

'I was just remembering last Easter. I had no idea then that in less than a year I would be a husband and a father, and very, very happy with the arrangement.'

Georgia smiled. 'That makes two of us.' She tipped her head back to look at him. 'Do I take it that your views on marriage have undergone a change, then?'

'Now that Carlo is here and you are safe and well in my arms marriage is everything I could wish for,' he assured her. 'Is it the same for you, my heart?'

'Yes, darling, it is.' Georgia pulled away a little to look at him rather warily. 'Though sometimes I shiver at how close I came to rejecting it all.'

Luca frowned. 'I do not understand.'

'I didn't have to marry you,' she said, her eyes falling.

'No,' he said grimly. 'I know that. You were prepared to bring our child up alone.'

'I wouldn't have had to do that, either. After—after you made love to me that day I wrote to James immediately, ending our relationship. He refused to accept it, so once I knew I was expecting your baby I wrote telling him so. But James still wanted to marry me, even offered to help me bring up the child—'

'*Cosa*?' Luca stared at her in outrage. 'He wanted to steal you *and* my son?'

'If there was any stealing, Luca Valori, it was the other way round,' said Georgia severely. 'And it was very good of James.'

Luca said something violent and extremely rude about James Astin, glaring at his wife, who smiled at him, unmoved.

'You've missed the point, Luca. I'm trying to tell you I *chose* to marry you.'

Luca pulled her to him with sudden ferocity, his mouth bruising hers with a kiss of such possession that Georgia pushed at him in protest until his arms slackened and his mouth softened, and then she returned the kiss with the response only he could ignite in her.

'It is well you chose me,' he said raggedly, when he raised his head. 'I would not have rested until you became my wife, Georgia.'

'I didn't really *choose* you. From the moment I first saw you there was never really any choice at all,' she said, burying her face against his shoulder.

'Then why did you fight me that afternoon?' he demanded, incensed.

'Because you obviously wanted me for another playmate. And I wanted so much more than that.' Her head tipped back and she raised a wry eyebrow at him. 'Which I got, well and truly, didn't I?'

'Are you sorry?' he asked imperiously.

'No. You know I'm not,' she whispered, kissing him.

'Then let us go to bed before Carlo wakes to demand his mother. It has been so long, my darling. I need you so much more than he does at this moment.' Luca stood up, holding out his hand. 'Come. I would carry you, but—'

'I'm not as sylph-like as I once was,' said Georgia, smothering a laugh as they went to peep at their son, who lay sleeping like an angel, the afternoon sunlight haloing his small, blond head.

'Very true,' Luca whispered, and drew her along the landing to their room, where he drew the russet curtains, enclosing the room in a warm, intimate glow. 'Also I wish to conserve all my energies for more fulfilling activities.' He sat down on the edge of the bed, pulling her between his knees so that he could bury his face between the ripe curves of her breasts.

Georgia's head went back, her eyes closed to savour the exquisite sensation of his lips; then they were locked in each other's arms on the bed, feverish in their need of each other.

'I want you so much, *carissima*,' groaned Luca, then gazed into her brilliant eyes. 'This is truly allowed now? The consultant made this plain to you?'

'Yes—yes—yes!' Georgia yielded exultantly as Luca began kissing her with a lack of restraint made fiercer by the abstinence of the last months, both of them catching fire so quickly that long before either of them had intended they were engulfed in the white heat of physical reunion without any preliminaries other than their intense need of each other.

Afterwards, still holding her cruelly tight in his arms, Luca raised his head and looked down into his wife's dark, dazed eyes.

'I feel sorry for this James Astin of yours.'

She smiled sleepily. 'I don't believe you.'

He ran the tip of his tongue over her bruised mouth. 'I mean it. To lose such joy as this—he is to be pitied.'

'You can't lose what you've never had!' Georgia smoothed his hair back from his damp forehead. 'There was never anything like this with James or anyone else. The "joy", as you put it, only happens with you, Luca.'

His eyes gleamed in triumph. 'This is true?'

'Yes.' Georgia eyed him quizzically. 'For you, of course, it's different.'

'Yes. It is. Utterly different.' He smiled, his fingers playing with a lock of her hair. 'I have made love to women before. You know that. But no one has ever brought me to such desperation of longing as you. And the others I just slept with and played with, Georgia. You are my life.'

For a moment she was speechless, her throat thickened with tears at the passionate sincerity of his declaration. She sniffed, blinked the tears away and smiled up into the brilliant blue gaze with the mischievous grin she knew he adored. 'I'm glad to hear it, Luca Valori.'

He smiled back. 'Why? It is so good to know you have tamed me so well?'

Georgia gave a hoot of laughter. '*Tame* you—that'll be the day!'

'Then why are you glad?'

'Because you're *my* life too,' she assured him, and melted into a crushing embrace which only slackened when an imperious, unmistakable cry came from the next room. 'Oh, dear, the other Valori male demanding attention! I'll be back soon—don't go away.'

Luca lay with his hands behind his head, watching her wrap herself in the white towelling robe she wore these days instead of the amber silk peignoir. 'Bring him in here. I love to watch you nurse him.'

Georgia blew him a kiss then raced off to see to her roaring son, who quieted a little as she changed him, his blue eyes so much like his father's that she hugged him tenderly as she carried him back to the other room.

Luca took the baby from her, waited until Georgia was settled comfortably against the pillows, then handed Carlo back, guiding him to the source of nourishment with a loving hand which lingered a little on the full, satiny curve before leaving the field clear for his son.

'That's a very thoughtful look,' said Georgia softly after a while, and he smiled at her.

'It just occurred to me that at one time my only ambition was to be world champion. At times I suppose I risked my life for it, yet now it seems so unimportant.'

She gave a little shiver. 'I'm glad I didn't know you then.'

'Why? Because of all my adoring fans?' he teased.

'No.' Georgia flipped her son up on her shoulder and patted his back. 'Because I love you so much, Luca Valori, I'd be in agony every time you were on the track.' She breathed in deeply and cradled the baby to her breast again. 'I can't bear to think of it.'

Luca reached over the downy fair head to kiss her. '*Dio*, how lucky I am. I took what I wanted that fateful afternoon with you—'

'Ah, but look what you had to pay for it!' she teased, returning the kiss.

He smiled triumphantly. 'My hand, my heart—my life, *tesoro*. A small price to pay for such a prized possession!'

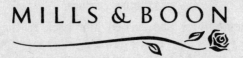

MILLS & BOON

Next Month's Romances

Each month you can choose from a wide variety of romance with Mills & Boon. Below are the new titles to look out for next month.

MISCHIEF AND MARRIAGE	Emma Darcy
DESERT MISTRESS	Helen Bianchin
RECKLESS CONDUCT	Susan Napier
RAUL'S REVENGE	Jacqueline Baird
DECEIVED	Sara Craven
DREAM WEDDING	Helen Brooks
THE DUKE'S WIFE	Stephanie Howard
PLAYBOY LOVER	Lindsay Armstrong
SCARLET LADY	Sara Wood
THE BEST MAN	Shannon Waverly
AN INCONVENIENT HUSBAND	Karen van der Zee
WYOMING WEDDING	Barbara McMahon
SOMETHING OLD, SOMETHING NEW	
	Catherine Leigh
TIES THAT BLIND	Leigh Michaels
BEGUILED AND BEDAZZLED	Victoria Gordon
SMOKE WITHOUT FIRE	Joanna Neil

Available from WH Smith, John Menzies, Volume One, Forbuoys, Martins, Woolworths, Tesco, Asda, Safeway and other paperback stockists.